LOSING HOPE

MICHELLE WINDSOR

Chapter One

H ope Yorke was not having a good morning. It started when her alarm clock didn't go off, causing her to bolt upright in bed when the doorman called to let her know her car had arrived. After the fastest shower ever, and the heaviest morning traffic in ages, things only got worse. Just as she walked out of Starbucks, some asshole slammed into her, causing her scalding hot latte to spill down the front of her black Donna Karan wrap dress and drip all the way down onto her brand new pink satin Louboutin heels.

She had waited three months for those shoes to come in on back order from Paris. Thankfully, she always kept several spare outfits in her office, so after another quick shower and change of clothes—a royal blue Calvin Klein belted Ponte knit dress with a black pair of Jimmy Choo suede pumps—she walked into the company board meeting quite late, a meeting in which her father sat at the head of the table. Taking her seat to his right, she didn't miss the look of disappointment that flashed across his stern features as he nodded to her.

"Nice of you to join us, Hope."

"My apologies to you all." She glanced around the table, making eye contact with each board member at the table. She may be the boss's daughter, but she expected no special treatment and had earned her right to sit at this table. Hope had graduated with honors from Columbia University with a major in Business Management and a minor in English and Comparative Literature, and for the last six years, she had worked her way up through the ranks of her father's publishing company. At only twenty-eight years old, she was proud to be the youngest ever Senior Vice President of US Publishing to sit at this table.

"I had a small accident on my way in this morning."

Her father's hand immediately reached out and covered hers as he asked quietly, "Are you all right, Hope?"

She nodded and smiled at him in return. "Yes, Father, I'm fine." She patted his hand and then, addressing the board, continued, "If someone will just catch me up, let's continue with the meeting."

The meeting lasted well past lunch and into the afternoon, so by the time Hope was back in her office, she had endless emails and messages to return. She was off to her lake house in Vermont that evening, and the sooner she could get through things, the sooner she could get on the road.

Several hours later, Emily, Hope's assistant, stood in the entrance to her office. "Excuse me, Miss Yorke, it's after five. Billy is on the phone and wants to know if you'll still require the helicopter this evening, or if you've changed your mind about heading North?"

"Shit!" Jumping up, she gathered her computer and paperwork and stuffed them into her bag. "I had no idea it had gotten so late! Yes, please ask Billy to wait, and can you also have Ed bring the car around to the front? It's faster if we leave from there instead of the garage entrance."

"Of course, Miss Yorke." Emily was out the door and back at her desk making the necessary calls before Hope could say another word.

Quickly pulling on her trench coat, she grabbed her bags and headed to take the elevator down to the lobby as fast as her heels would allow. She walked outside into the chilly fall air to find Ed waiting for her at the curb beside the car. He tipped his head in greeting. "Miss Yorke. Seaport Helipad?"

Giving him a nod, she handed him her computer bag. "Yes, please, Ed, the quicker the better. I completely lost track of time."

She climbed into the back as he closed the door behind her. The car carried a light scent of the Old Spice aftershave he always wore, which Hope thought was better than any air freshener that could have been used. She heard him load her bag into the trunk, and then he was in the driver's seat and pulling smoothly into traffic. "I'll get you there as quick as I can, Miss. Traffic's a little heavy right now, it being Friday night and all."

"Thank you again, Ed. Billy's waiting at the helipad for me, so I appreciate it."

"Just you going up North this weekend, Miss?" Weathered blue eyes looked at her in question from the rear-view mirror.

"Yep, just me. Need a bit of a break from everything."

Ed knew it was a little more than that. He knew that almost two weeks ago she'd come back early from a business trip and, instead of going home, had decided to surprise her boyfriend of two years at his place. The surprise was on her, though, when she walked in and found him screwing some redhead on the kitchen counter. Ed knew this because he was behind her with her bags. He was also the one to cold-cock that prick Dylan in the chin when he ran after her as she turned and fled. He then listened to her cry in the backseat of the car as he drove her back to her apartment. Yeah, Ed knew she needed a little break all right.

They reached the heliport, and Ed helped her out of the car and grabbed her computer bag from the trunk. After entering the terminal and confirming their identities, Ed walked with Hope to the helipad where Billy was waiting next to the helicopter. He smiled wide at Hope and nodded to Ed in greeting as he walked out to meet them.

"We're all set to go, Miss Yorke. I'm sorry I can't take you all the way up this time. Tower says the rain and wind are a bit too strong to take the chopper."

"It's no problem at all, Billy. At least we can still take the plane." Hope was getting seated in the chopper now, with Billy making sure her straps were buckled securely. He circled around the chopper, hopped in on his side, and strapped himself in.

"It should be a quick fifteen minutes over to the airport. The plane is ready and waiting for you at the terminal."

Hope nodded in acknowledgment as the chopper took flight over the river and then banked to the left toward LaGuardia. These were the perks of being a Yorke. Hope had private helicopters and planes to take her wherever she needed to go, when she wanted to go, and this weekend, all she wanted was some time to herself. She was looking forward to curling up with a book in front of the fire, drinking wine, sleeping late, going for long walks around the lake, and just forgetting about the last couple of weeks.

What a prick Dylan turned out to be. She knew she wasn't in love him and probably wouldn't ever have married him. But still, what happened to having a little respect and just breaking things off with someone, instead of cheating on them? They were supposed to be damn grownups, after all. Humiliation still burned in her gut. Of course, within hours, there were endless deliveries of flowers and calls from Dylan asking for forgiveness. After one phone call back, calmly telling him to go fuck himself, or better yet, the redhead, she threw herself into her work, putting in sixteen-hour days to try to numb the pain of her new reality. That was almost two weeks ago, and the long days had caught up with her.

As promised, fifteen minutes later, they landed at LaGuardia. A shuttle was waiting to drive her over to the private terminal where the company jet was housed. Upon arrival, she boarded the plane and made herself comfortable in one of the white leather seats.

"Good evening, Miss Yorke. It's nice to see you." Sylvia, one of the regular flight attendants on board, seemed to appear from nowhere, ready to make sure Hope was comfortable and didn't need anything.

"Hello, Sylvia. Nice to see you, as well. Do you think you could get me some coffee?"

"Of course. Are you hungry? I can make you anything on the menu."

"Just the coffee for now. Thank you."

Sylvia smiled and made her way to the small galley.

The Captain boarded the plane and greeted Hope with a warm smile. "All pre-checks are done, Miss. We can leave as soon as the tower gives us clearance."

"Wonderful, Glenn. Thank you." Sylvia appeared and handed Hope a mug of freshly brewed coffee, of course, prepared exactly to her liking, and then disappeared back in the galley.

"There's a pretty good storm going on from Montpelier and up through Canada, so things may get a little bumpy at the tail end of our flight."

Her brow furrowed. "Any reason to be concerned or delay my flight?"

"We'll get you there no problem. Your father would have my neck in a noose if I did anything to harm his most precious asset." He gave her a friendly wink and headed to the cockpit.

Several minutes later, they were in the air and leaving the island of Manhattan behind. She felt lighter and lighter as the distance between her and the city grew. Going up to the lake house was her sanctuary, and she couldn't wait to get there. Her grandfather had built the house on Lake Champlain over seventy years ago. It wasn't an extravagant house in any way. In fact, it was the complete opposite of what her home and life were like in the city. The lake house was rustic, all wood and stone and everything a house on a country lake should be.

The first floor was one big open space that contained the kitchen, dining, and living room. The entire back side of the living room wall was made up of windows that overlooked a huge deck and, of course, the beautiful lake. There was a stone fireplace that made up one side wall in the living room and was surrounded by big, over-stuffed sofas. The sofas were strewn with throw pillows and lap blankets made of the softest fabrics. She loved to sit on those couches for hours just staring out at the lake, watching the world swim by.

Upstairs were four bedrooms, one on each corner of the house, with a bathroom on each side, between each room. The beds were still covered with quilts that Hope's grandmother had made by hand. Soft, thick rugs were on the wooden floors of each room, helping to keep toes warm on cold winter mornings. The master bedroom faced the lake and had another stone fireplace along the wall.

The only rooms in the house to be updated had been the bathrooms. Until she was around three, only cold water ran through the house, and the plumbing was limited. Her father had made it a priority to update the plumbing and bathroom fixtures, more for his comfort than anyone else's. Her mother had grown up at the lake house, so it had never bothered her. Her father did stay true to the style of the house, outfitting the bathrooms with beautiful claw foot bath tubs and antique vanities. The first time her mother took a hot bubble bath in one of the huge tubs, she had declared that perhaps this time her husband had been right.

Forty-five minutes later, a bit of turbulence jarred the plane, signaling their arrival at the edge of the storm. She sat up straighter, pulled her seatbelt tight, and prepared herself for a bumpy ride. When she lifted the shade on the window, splatters of wind-driven rain hit the glass, blackened by the night sky.

"We'll be landing in about twenty minutes, but it will be a rough few minutes. Can I get you anything before I buckle in?" Sylvia had magically appeared again.

"No, I'm fine. Thank you." She watched Sylvia sway back and forth from the turbulence as she made her way back to the front of the plane to secure herself for the rest of the flight.

She wasn't afraid of flying but wasn't particularly fond of being on a plane bouncing through the air at thirty thousand feet. She clutched onto the arm rests and counted the minutes until she heard the plane's landing gear descend. A few more drops and vicious sways, and the plane finally bounced onto the runway, wing flaps up and brakes squealing. Looking out the window again, Hope saw that the rain was pouring down and blowing sideways from the power of the wind. The plane slowly made its way to a private hanger, where it parked, a dry shelter from the storm.

Her Range Rover was parked in the hanger, and she thanked her lucky stars that she had driven it up here the last time she had visited. Her Mercedes S-Coupe wouldn't have handled the weather very well, but she had no doubt the Rover could. She unbuckled and gratefully accepted her trench coat from Sylvia.

"Are you sure you want to drive to the house in this weather, Miss Yorke? Maybe it would be better for you to stay in town tonight until the storm passes?" Sylvia questioned with nothing but concern.

"I'll be just fine." Smiling warmly, she patted her on the shoulder. "I have the Range Rover, and I know the roads like the back of my hand."

"Well, all right then. Will we be seeing you again for the ride back, or will you be driving down?"

"I haven't decided yet, but I'll make sure to let the team know by Sunday. I won't be leaving until Monday at the earliest."

Sylvia handed over her computer bag and purse then walked with her to the door. It had been opened and the stairs lowered for her exit.

"All right, Miss, please drive carefully, and as always, nothing but the best wishes for you."

"Thank you." Hope gave her a warm smile and started down the stairs. Glenn was waiting at the bottom to greet her.

"Sorry about the rough landing. Damn winds fought us every step of the way." He shook his head in frustration.

"Glenn, it was fine. We're all here in one piece." She walked toward the Rover.

"Well, the keys are in the Range Rover, and it's all gassed up for you. Maggie already stocked the house for you, so you should be fine once you get there."

"Wonderful. I'm not sure about my return plans yet, but

I'll let you and your team know as soon as I decide." Opening the rear door, she placed her computer bag and purse in the seat, taking her cell phone out to keep in the front with her.

"Very good. You just enjoy your time here, and we'll be ready if you need us."

"Thanks so much, Glenn." She gave him a quick peck on the cheek and climbed in behind the steering wheel.

"You be careful on those roads, Hope." He shut the door, hit the roof once with his palm, and walked away.

With a push of a button, the Rover roared to life, and she backed out of the hanger and headed toward the airport exit. The wipers were on at full blast as the rain pelted down and the wind whipped leaves and debris up from the road. Under normal circumstances, it generally took about thirty minutes to get to the lake house, but given the weather, she knew it might take longer. She hoped that the power hadn't been knocked out. It was a common occurrence around the lake when the weather turned bad.

She saw the sign for the highway entrance and merged to the right to enter. The highway was dark and wet, without another vehicle in sight. It was only a little after nine o'clock, but people must have been smarter than her, already at their homes, dry, and warm. The wipers continued to swish quickly back and forth, working hard to keep her view clear. She only had to be on the highway for one exit, but this far North, exits were about ten miles apart from each other. Reaching down, she turned the radio on but got nothing but static, so she hit the CD button and scrolled through until the fourth CD came up. "Round

Here" by the Counting Crows started playing over the speakers, and she sang along. This disc was one of her favorites and hadn't been taken out of the Rover since she purchased it.

Soon enough, she reached the exit and pulled off to merge onto Route 2. She was halfway to the house now, but this is where the roads got a little trickier. It was a simple two-lane road, curvy, and there wasn't a street light for miles. She knew the road well, though, and continued to sing her heart out as she drove through the storm, feeling safe in the sturdy SUV. Another fifteen minutes and she'd be there.

Chapter Two

Gage Flynn was not having a good night. He was stuck in the middle of bum-fucking-nowhere, in a shitty rental car that died and wouldn't restart. He tried for over an hour to get the thing running again, in the pouring rain, but no luck. And because he was in the middle of bum-fucking-nowhere, his cell phone had no reception. He was sitting in the car—wet, hungry, and pissed off—wishing someone would drive by and actually stop for him. He was losing hope. After sitting there for almost an hour, not a single car had gone by. He was sure the weather had everyone tucked in their houses for the night. So, now, he was trying to dry off in the car in hopes of getting warm, but his stomach wouldn't stop grumbling. Lunch was the last meal he'd eaten, and it was almost nine o'clock now. It was going to be a long fucking night.

He may not have reception on his phone, but he could still listen to music. He scrolled down to one of his favorite playlists, the Counting Crows, and hit play. He was in the middle of belting out "Rain King", ironically, when an SUV came around the corner and almost ran into the back of his car. The driver slammed on the brakes and skidded to a stop, just inches from Gage's stalled rental car. He peered back and could see her hands clutching the steering wheel as she stared straight ahead, eyes wide with shock. Gage threw his driver's side door open, jumped out, and ran over, grabbing the handle of her door to open it. He pointed down to the lock and yelled, "Unlock the door!"

Frightened, the woman shook her head no at the same time as she yelled the word. Gage yelled at her through the window, "Are you all right?"

He couldn't understand why she wouldn't open the damn door. It was pouring out, for God's sake, and he just wanted to make sure she was okay.

Pushing the electric window button, allowing it to open an inch, she yelled out, "I'm fine! What the hell are you doing in the middle of the road?"

"Sorry! Damn rental broke down, and I have no cell reception. Do you have a phone?"

Looking down at her phone, she frowned and held up the dark phone to him. She yelled back through her window, "I'm sorry, it's dead. I'll call Triple A when I get to my house. It's only a few miles down the road."

He shook his head, drops flying from his hair, as he tried to wipe away the water running down his face. "Seriously? It's pouring rain out here. Can you just give me a ride?"

He could see the wheels turning in her head as she tried to decide whether or not to give this stranger a ride. "Listen,

I'm a nice guy. I promise! Just a ride to a phone and you won't ever have to see me again!"

~

"Isn't that what all serial murderers say?" she yelled back through the window. Even looking like a drowned rat, she couldn't help but notice this guy was seriously good looking. Didn't Ted Bundy lure woman this way, too?

"I'm freezing here, lady. I give you my word on the bible that I'm not a bad guy."

She looked down, gnawing on her lower lip, wondering if she'd end up another sad story on the news of a missing woman if she let him in. But the poor guy was soaked to the skin, shaking and shivering in the rain. Her compassion for his predicament overtook her common sense.

"Okay, but you better be telling me the truth!" She flipped the switch and unlocked the doors.

"Thank you! Let me just grab my bags from the car and lock it." As the man moved back to the rental car, she watched as he grabbed a black duffel, what looked to be a camera bag, and the keys from the ignition, then lock the door and run back. He opened the rear door first, depositing his gear, and then opened the passenger side door, finally getting in and slamming the door.

"Thanks again. I've been here almost two hours." She looked over to him with what must have been shock written on her face. He looked down, taking in the water dripping from him and onto her Italian leather seats. His gaze swung back to her, and he shrugged apologetically. "Sorry."

"I know, I know." He must have thought she was aghast at his impression of a drowned rat, but she was actually stupefied by the way his wet clothes clung to his skin, outlining his muscular frame. She shook her head to clear it. "I'm sorry, I know it's just water. It will dry."

"I'm Gage Flynn, by the way." He held out his hand to her, but she just looked at its wet, dripping form and gave him a short wave instead, her eyes raking over his features, taking in the way his green eyes crinkled when he smiled.

"I'm Hope. Where should I bring you?"

"You tell me. It's not my town at all. I was just here for the day shooting a wedding and was trying to get to the airport to catch a flight out tomorrow morning."

"Well, I just came from the airport, and I can tell you that not one place appeared to be open when I drove through. You don't know anyone around here? I really don't want to drive back to the airport." She sighed tiredly.

"No one. I'm sorry. Listen, do you have a regular phone line at your place? I can—"

She held her hand up to stop him from talking. "You want to come to my house now? Are you crazy? I don't even know you. This is how every horror movie starts, and we both know how they end."

His brow furrowed, and he shook his head in frustration. "Listen, Hope, right?"

She nodded her head. "Yes."

"First off, I'm fucking starving. I haven't eaten in almost ten hours. I'm soaking wet, I'm freezing, and I'm tired. The last thing I want to do, or have the energy to do, is rape, hurt, or murder you. You're a beautiful woman, but really, it's the last thing on my mind. All I want to do is find a phone, call a tow, get some dry clothes, and eat something." He took his hand and slicked his dripping, shoulder-length hair back away from his face and looked down in exasperation.

Moving her eyes over his frame, she took in his soaked condition, saw he was shivering from the cold and rain, and realized in that instant what a complete bitch she was being.

"Okay, let's go then." Reaching over, she turned the heat and blowers on his side of the vehicle to high. She then put the Rover in gear and pulled out around his car to start back down the road. "I'm sorry I don't have anything dry to give you. I just got in from New York and keep clothes at the house, so no suitcase."

He smiled. "No worries, really. I'm just happy you came along. I was afraid I was going to be spending the night there."

Opening the center console, she pulled out a granola bar and handed it to him with a smile. "I do have this, though. It hasn't been in there that long."

"Oh my God! Thank you!" Snagging it from her, he tore the wrapper off and inhaled half the bar in one bite as a groan rolled out of his mouth.

Looking at him out of the corner of her eye, she noticed how his hair was starting to curl up a bit on the edges as it was drying. "Okay, so I don't think there's going to be anywhere between here and where I live that will be open. We are in Vermont, after all."

He looked over at her and gave her a look that basically said, *no shit.*

"We have a landline at my house, so we'll give Triple A a call when we get there and see what they say about getting you a tow. Okay?"

"Sounds perfect. Really, I can't thank you enough." Reaching over, he grasped her forearm in a quick squeeze of thanks. His touch felt hot and electric, causing her to jump in surprise.

"Sorry, did I hurt you?" His eyes squinted as his brow furrowed again.

She laughed lightly. 'No, no. Sorry, just jumpy." She could still feel tingles on her arm where he had touched her. *When was the last time a man gave her tingles from a single touch?*

"Are you getting warmer yet?" Her trench coat was still on, and even though she had only turned the heat up on his side, a bead of sweat trickled slowly down her back.

"It feels amazing." He looked over and must have realized she looked a little flushed. "Too warm for you, though?"

She shook her head. "No, it's okay. Keep it on. Let's see if we can dry you off a little bit."

"You're just worried about these leather seats, aren't you?"

Looking over at him, she feigned a shocked expression. "The thought never even crossed my mind!"

Laughing loudly, he joked, "Come on! I saw the horror on your face when I first jumped in. What's this sucker run, a hundred grand?"

"What? Isn't that kind of rude to ask someone?" She

laughed nervously. *What if this was actually a setup and he knew she was rich?* "Besides, I didn't pay for it. My father did. I'm more worried about his reaction to the water stains and how I'm going to explain them."

His expression darkened a bit at the mention of her father. "Oh, I get it now. You're a daddy's girl."

"Excuse me?" Her eyes went wide.

He just shook his head. "Never mind. Sorry I said anything. Really, I'm just hungry and cranky."

She turned off the main road and started down the dirt road that led to the house. The drive was only about half a mile long, but it wasn't lit, and it was lined with trees, so she drove slowly.

"We're almost there." No sooner than the words were out of her mouth, she was slamming on the brakes again. A tree had fallen in the road, right in their path.

"Shit." She turned and looked at him. "Now what?"

"We move it. That's what."

Brows shot up over her weary eyes. "How in the world do we move that? It's too big for us to push out of the way."

He smiled wide, eyes crinkling again. "Not too big for this fancy Range Rover, though."

She looked at him again questioningly. "What?"

He shook his head. "You didn't notice it has a wench on the front of it?"

"A what?"

Laughing, he reached for the door handle. "Yep, you're a city girl, all right." He opened the door and jumped out. "Just stay put, but leave it running and the lights on for me."

She watched as he moved in front of the Rover and

began pulling on something before climbing up and over the tree, wrapping some kind of wire around it as he went. Curiosity got the best of her, and even though the rain was still pouring down, she opened the door and stepped outside. Her heels immediately sunk in the mud of the dirt driveway, and she cursed the fact that another pair of her beautiful shoes were getting ruined in one day. She pulled her heels up and walked on the balls of her feet over to the tree to see what he was doing.

"Gage!" she yelled at the tree because she could only see the wire. His head popped up from behind the tree.

"What are you doing? I told you to stay put." He jumped back over the tree and walked over to her. "Now, you're soaking wet, too. Get back inside!" He grasped her arm and starting leading her back. When he tried to turn her, he noticed she was walking on her tippy-toes. He looked down in question and pointed to her feet.

"What the hell are you doing?" They had to yell each time they spoke so they could be heard above the wind and the rain.

"My heels keep sinking in the mud!"

He just shook his head, and before she could say another word, he scooped her up and carried her over to the passenger side of the Rover.

"Hey! What are you doing?" She grasped onto his shoulders, clinging tightly, noticing how firm the muscles that lay under the wet shirt were, and tried not to enjoy how he was holding her.

"This is faster. Just go with it." Opening the door with

one hand, he placed her in the seat. "Besides, I need to drive for this part so I can pull the tree out of the way."

Before she could object, he shut the door, ran around, and jumped into the driver's seat. He flipped a switch on the dash, and she heard a motor turn on and saw the tree jerk. He shifted into reverse and slowly started backing up, pulling the tree with him out of the road. When the tree was out of the way enough for them to be able to drive around it, he put it back in park. He flipped another switch on the dash, and she heard the motor turn on again. She looked at him questioningly.

"Loosening the wire. Be right back." He jumped out, and she watched as he removed the wire from around the tree. She heard some clanging and then saw him lean up over the hood and smile at her through the rain and wind. Her heart did a little flip. What kind of guy could smile after being stuck on the side of the road for hours, with no food, and then moving a tree in a rain storm?

He jumped back in and turned, still smiling. "Bet you're glad you picked me up now, aren't you?" He flipped the switch to the motor one more time to reel the wire back in.

She nodded gratefully. "More than you know. Can we call this karma? A good deed coming back around?"

"Maybe." He put the Rover back in drive and maneuvered around the tree, continuing the rest of the way down the road.

A minute later, the house came into view, and Hope breathed a huge sigh of relief. She pointed to a spot next to an old pickup truck already parked against the side of the house.

"You can park right over there." He pulled into the place she indicated and shut off the engine.

"Home sweet home?" he asked curiously.

"Weekend home sweet home. I live in New York. This is where I come when I want to escape the craziness for a while."

They opened their doors, both of them grabbing their own bags, and then ran up onto the covered porch out of the rain.

"The red key on the ring is for the deadbolt." She pointed to the keys that were in his hand. He pulled open the screen door and then, putting the key in the lock, turned and opened the door. He held the door for Hope to go in first. She walked in and flipped the switches to the right of the door, but nothing happened. She flipped them on and off again, expecting different results, but of course, nothing.

"Shit. No power." He walked in and shut the door behind him. He was dripping wet and shivering again.

"Candles?" he asked her.

"Yes, we have oil lamps. It's not unusual to lose power during storms up here." She pulled her jacket off and slipped out of her muddy shoes before hanging the jacket on one of a row of hooks stationed behind the front door.

"Stay right here. I'm going to light a lamp and get you a towel."

"Okay, staying put." He held up his hands in surrender, like he was afraid to get anything else of hers wet. She padded off down the hall.

Even though it was dark in the house, Hope knew it like the back of her hand and had no problem moving about to get a lamp lit. She walked through the kitchen to the attached pantry and, feeling with her fingers, found a lamp on the top shelf. She carried it to the counter next to the stove, opened one of the drawers, and pulled out a long wooden match. Lifting the glass shade of the lamp enough to get the match in, she struck the match against the slate on the counter, igniting it, and then held it against the wick. It caught, and light immediately flooded from the lamp, so she closed the shade and turned the flame up to brighten it.

Holding the lamp, she went quickly to one of the upstairs bathrooms and grabbed a couple towels for Gage. When she walked back down and into the hallway, he was pacing back and forth.

"We have light!" She handed him the towels, which he took gratefully.

"If you want to take those wet clothes off and leave them there, I can find you something of my brother's to wear. Does that sound good?"

He nodded his head. "That sounds amazing. I'm freezing, and the only thing in my bags is a suit and some cameras."

"Okay, hold tight. I'll go find something for you." She turned and walked off and was about to walk back upstairs when she realized she left him in the dark again, so she went back to the kitchen and pulled several more oil lamps from the shelf in the pantry. She lit two, leaving one on the kitchen counter and then, carrying two lamps now, headed back to the hallway. Hope rounded the corner, lights blaring, to find Gage bent over, bare ass in the air, trying to pull his wet jeans off the bottom half of his body. His shirt was already off, so she couldn't help but notice the muscles rippling across his back from the effort of trying to get his soaked jeans off. She could also see he had several tattoos, but before she could look further, she cleared her throat to let him know she was there.

"Um, sorry." She bent down, placed the lamp on the floor, and started backing away, making sure to keep looking down. "I'm just going to leave this here for you."

~

Gage jerked his head up in surprise when he heard her clear her throat, quickly pulling one of the towels off the floor to try to cover his ass. He turned in time to see her setting down one of the lamps then slinking away and wondered how much she saw.

As if she had read his mind, she yelled out, "Don't worry! I didn't see a thing! Too dark!" Then he heard her footsteps as she ran up the stairs.

When he'd turned to find her standing there with the lamp, it was the first time he got a really good look at her and noticed what an attractive woman she was. She was wearing what he was sure was some expensive designer dress, in a dark color that offset the pale color of her skin. It was belted tightly around her small waist, accenting the curve of her hips. The back of the dress had a slit that allowed him to see her long legs as she walked away. Her blonde hair was wrapped up in a ball at the base of her neck, but he would bet when it was undone, it was long. She was definitely in a different league than him.

After finally peeling his jeans off, he hung them and his

dripping shirt on the hooks behind the door. He placed one of the towels under the dripping clothes to capture the water then took the other and wrapped it around his waist, securing it tightly. Walking over to the lamp, he picked it up and wandered down the hallway. He stopped in amazement at the space that lay before him.

It was a huge open room that was filled with big comfy couches, bookcases, and an enormous stone fireplace. Off to the left was a kitchen that looked like it could cook for an army if required. But it was the wall of windows that captured his attention. Even though it was dark, he could see the lake on the other side of the glass, rain splattering the water and waves crashing into the shore. He imagined it must be beautiful on a day when the sun was shining. The sound of pattering feet had him turning back around to see her as she reached the bottom of the stairs.

"Oh!" She seemed startled to see him in the living room. "Sorry, I didn't expect to see you in here."

"Did you want me to wait in the hallway like a dog?" he asked her jokingly.

"No, of course not." He couldn't help notice how she stared at his chiseled chest and stomach, a dusting of light brown hair covering his pecs leading down to what he knew was a well-defined waist. He had that V thing women seemed to love, that started at his hips and dipped below the edge of his towel, and his tattoos were on display. He had a large Celtic cross on his upper left arm and, on his right side, a tribal tattoo that started on the back side and wrapped around his shoulder and down part of his arm. The word Faith was written over his heart, too, but with the angle he was standing, he doubted she could see it clear enough to make it out.

She held out the clothes she had taken from her brother's room. "Here you go. It's just a pair of sweats and a t-shirt, but they're dry."

He walked forward and took them from her. He pulled the t-shirt over his head and thought he heard her groan. Grabbing the sweats, he started pulling them on under the towel.

"Whoa! What are you doing?" She held out her hands and then turned around, trying to cover her eyes with her free hand.

"What?" He looked up in surprise, saw her embarrassment, and laughed. "Don't worry, I'm not taking the towel off until I'm covered."

She stammered, "I barely know you!"

"Which is why I'm putting some clothes back on. I do believe I made a promise not to rape or murder you."

She spun around at that, looking relieved to see he was dressed again. "Not funny."

He laughed out loud. "You're a skittish thing, aren't you?"

"No, I'm not." She put her hands on her hips and stuck her chest out defiantly. "But you are a complete stranger to me. I'm not used to strange men getting naked in front of me."

"I wasn't naked." He smiled again. "Thank you very much for the dry clothes. Phone?"

She looked at him and gave him an apologetic frown. "Out. Sorry, no power means no phone, and without power,

I can't charge my cell phone. Did you check to see if yours has reception?"

"Yeah, I checked when you were getting me the clothes. Not a single bar."

Her eyes narrowed, and a small frown fell on her lips. "Okay, not a rapist or murderer, right?"

"Right. Still a no."

"Okay, well, I can't very well throw you out in the storm, and there is no way I'm driving you all the way back to town. So, I guess you're staying here for the night."

Looking her in the eye and nodding slowly, Gage asked, "You sure you're okay with that?"

"I've got a lock on my door, and I'll sleep with a knife under my pillow, too." She winked at him as she said this.

A wide grin broke across his face. "Thanks. Really, I appreciate this."

She held up her hands in defeat and shrugged. "Well, there's not much else we can do, so it is what it is. Plus, you rescued me in the end with the whole tree mess, so who really ended up being the hero here?"

He pretended to puff out his chest. "Course I did. That's what us heroes do."

They both laughed. She walked over to the counter and grabbed one of the oil lamps. "I'm going to go change. The kitchen was stocked this morning, so you should be able to find anything you need in the fridge. I don't know how long the power's been out, though, so just be careful, I guess. The pantry has wine, too, if you want a glass."

She started walking toward the stairs and then turned around. "Do you know how to light a fire?"

"Yep." He grinned broadly. "Earned my boy scout badge for it and everything."

"Wonderful. Would you mind starting one for us? The furnace is gas, but it still needs electricity to run, and it might help to keep the house warm for us tonight."

"No problem." He walked toward the huge fireplace.

"Kindling, matches, and wood should all be stocked over there. Thanks so much." With that, she walked up the stairs.

Chapter Three

Hope walked into her big master bedroom and shut the door behind her. She knew she should probably be nervous about having this strange man in her house, but she just wasn't. There was something about him that seemed right to her, and it wasn't just how good he looked with his damn clothes off. She realized she wanted to spend more time with him. He made her laugh, and damn, the man turned the tables and ended up rescuing her, making it look easy as he did it. If she had to really be honest with herself, she definitely liked how it felt when his arms had scooped her up and held her. Maybe some time with another man was just what she needed.

She undid the belt around her waist and let out a long sigh. *Jesus, that felt good.* Unzipping the dress, she let it fall at her feet and then walked into the adjoining bathroom, taking the lamp with her. Knowing the hot water heater would have at least fifty gallons of hot water stored, she decided to take a chance on a really quick shower. She stripped out of her panties and bra and pulled her hair out of the bun she had it in.

Turning the water on, she stepped into the shower and let the cool water run over her. Not steaming hot, but still warm enough to get her feeling a bit refreshed. Hope quickly soaped up her hair, rinsed, conditioned, and then rinsed again. Grabbing her loofah, she squeezed on some body wash and scrubbed away the dirt from the day. One more rinse, and she shut the water off. She grabbed one of the towels off the rack and wrapped it around her hair, piling it up on top of her head. Taking another towel, she dried off and then applied some lotion to her skin.

Walking out into her bedroom, she found a comfy pair of black yoga pants and her favorite long-sleeved flannel shirt and pulled them both on. Whether she should wear a bra or not had her stalled for a moment, but she wasn't a huge breasted girl, and the flannel was thick and baggy, and really, she just wanted to be comfortable. Going back into the bathroom, she pulled the towel off her head and dried her hair the best she could. Brushing out the long, blond, curly locks, she decided to just keep it down.

She grabbed the oil lamp from the bathroom counter and made her way back downstairs. The sound of fire crackling reached her ears before she was even halfway down. The warm, smoky scent it always threw made her smile. She loved being here, power or not. As she turned into the kitchen, she could smell something else, as well. Gage was cooking?

He looked up as she entered the kitchen and smiled

warmly at her. "I hope you don't mind." He looked at the pan on the stove, currently filled with what looked like spaghetti sauce, and shrugged. "I figured it was the least I could do since you're stuck with me."

"Are you kidding? If you can cook, you can stay all weekend!" She laughed and walked over to the stove so she could get a better look at what was cooking. Yep, spaghetti. Her stomach grumbled, and she looked down at it in surprise.

"Guess I'm not the only one that's hungry." Gage held up a bottle of wine. "Do you want a glass?"

"God, yes!" Hope took the oil lamp she was holding and set it on one of the end tables in the living room.

"Fire, wine, and cooking! This is better than some dates I've been on," Hope joked as she walked back into the kitchen. He met her halfway and handed her the glass of wine, their fingertips brushing against each other in the process. The same surge of electricity and heat that his touch triggered earlier, tingled through her fingers, causing her to pull her hand back quickly, her eyes shooting up to meet his. His green eyes stared back, his expression intent.

She tore her eyes from his and walked past him toward the stove. "Do you need any help? Did you find everything okay?"

"I think I'm good. When I saw it was a gas range, I almost cried. You have no idea how hungry I am!"

Hope nodded. "For the longest time, when I was a little girl, there was a big cast iron woodstove that we did all the cooking on. Once my grandmother passed away, though, my father insisted on a putting a real stove in. My mother made him agree to gas, though, because she knew how often the power went out and wanted to make sure we could still cook if it did."

She moved over and sat on one of the bar stools that was on the other side of the stove.

~

Gage added spaghetti to the now boiling water and then turned the sauce down to low. After stirring the pasta, he came around the counter and sat next to Hope. He could smell her sweet yet spicy scent, almost like cinnamon but then citrusy. He was tempted to lean down and inhale more deeply, but he didn't want to frighten her.

"So, was it your mom or dad's mom who lived here?" He took a sip of his wine and watched her. He thought she looked amazing in the dress he saw her in earlier, but seeing her now, in her element, in a flannel shirt no less, with her long hair damp and curling down her back, no one had ever looked more beautiful to him. He wanted to reach out and run his fingers through her hair to see if was as soft as it looked.

"It was my mom's mom. My grandfather built this house for her, and my mom grew up here. When my grandmother died, she left it to my mother." Hope took a sip of her wine and then got up and walked around to stir the pasta again. The way she looked then was unnerving, and he wished he could see right through her and into her soul.

"So, someday, I guess your mom will leave it to you then, huh?" Gage asked.

Hope looked back at him with a sad look on her face. "It's already mine."

Gage got up and walked around the counter and up to her. "I'm sorry, Hope. You're so young, I just didn't even think."

She shrugged. "It's okay. How could you know?" She took another drink of her wine, emptying her glass, then picked up the bottle and refilled it before holding the bottle up in question to see if he wanted more. He nodded, so she refilled his glass, finishing off the bottle, and then went and sat back down.

"She died six years ago. A car accident. Right before I graduated from college."

She looked down into her wine glass and frowned. "I mean, it's been six years, but I still miss her every day. Life just isn't fair sometimes. I thank God for my brother. He took care of me and made sure I survived through it."

"Is your dad still alive, or was he with her?"

"No, he's still alive. He fell apart for a while after she died, though. He couldn't get past his own grief to help us with ours." She looked up with a sad smile on her face.

"It's better now. He's better now. He's a good father."

He looked at her for a long time, his face a blank mask, before replying, "I'm really sorry about your mother, Hope."

He checked the pasta then and smiled again, trying to move past the somber conversation they'd just had. "This is ready. Want to get some plates for us?"

"Sure." She got off the stool and started gathering the

plates and silverware they would need, as he drained the pasta in a colander that was already waiting in the sink. She set the table and then went into the pantry to grab salt, pepper, and napkins. She brought another bottle of wine, too, and left it sitting on the counter on her way back to the table.

He found a large bowl and began mixing the pasta and sauce together with some tongs. "I didn't put any meat in the sauce. I wasn't sure if you were a vegetarian or vegan or whatever."

"Nope, but thanks. I like my meat." Her face turned beet red at her comment, and his mind took the same dirty turn as hers.

Eyebrows raised, he just replied, smiling, "Good to know for future reference."

"Oh, do you plan on being around long enough to cook for me some more?" she jokingly replied. They had both sat down at the table now, and he began scooping pasta onto her plate. She held out her hand to indicate he had served enough.

"Well, you did say that I was the best date you'd had in a while." He scooped some of the pasta on his plate and then placed the bowl on the table. Picking up his glass and tipping it toward her, he smiled smugly. "Bon appetite!"

She clinked her glass against his and took another long sip of her wine. *Why did this feel so much like a date?* She had planned on a quiet weekend alone, and now, she was sitting here by lamp light, in her pajamas, drinking wine and eating dinner with a complete stranger. It didn't help that the stranger was pretty damn good looking and could cook, not to mention light a fire and drag trees out of the road. Did she mention how good he looked?

As if Gage could sense her looking at him, he raised his eyes up to meet hers and smiled. "How is it?"

Hope twirled some of the pasta onto her fork and scooped it into her mouth. "Hmmm." She hummed while chewing. "So good!"

He smiled broadly at the compliment and continued to eat. After they both had their fill, they sat at the table drinking the rest of the wine in their glasses.

"So, you said you were here shooting a wedding? You're a photographer then?"

He nodded his head in confirmation. "Yeah, I don't generally do weddings, but it was for a buddy of mine's brother who called in a favor."

"So, what do you normally photograph then?" She had finished her wine, so she got up, gathered their dirty dishes, and walked over to place them in the sink. She held up the wine bottle in question to see if he wanted more.

He shrugged his shoulders. "Sure, why not? Not driving anywhere. You want help opening the bottle?"

She grabbed the bottle opener off the counter. "No, thanks. I've got it."

After popping the cork, she carried the bottle over to the

table. "Want to go sit on the couches instead, over by the fire? It's a lot more comfy."

He stood up and grabbed both of their glasses. "Sure, sounds good to me. I think I'm still half-frozen from that rain."

He set the glasses down on the long coffee table in front of the couches and walked over to the fireplace. He removed the screen, threw a few more logs on the fire, and then replaced it. When he turned around, Hope was refilling both of their glasses. She picked them both up and walked over to stand in front of the fire with him, handing him his glass. This time, when their fingertips brushed, they both looked up, eyes meeting and holding.

"So, what kind of photography?" she spat out quickly, breaking eye contact before things got even stranger, and looked at the fire.

Gage wasn't sure anymore if it was the fire, the wine, or the way she just looked at him that was making him warm. He didn't think he was imagining the chemistry between them, and if the electric spark he felt when she handed him his wine was any indication, she was feeling it, too.

"Mostly freelance. I work for different publications, shooting whatever they need. I prefer outside shoots, more candid subjects, like animals, people and nature."

She nodded her head, still seemingly focused on the fire. "Any gallery showings? I'd love to see your work."

"I've had a couple. It's not my favorite thing, really. I like being behind the lens and having the attention focused on someone else."

Hope moved over and curled herself into the corner of the closest couch and then patted the seat next to her to indicate he should sit if he wanted. "Yes, I know a few photographers, and they all say the same thing."

He moved over to the couch and sat a few feet away from her. He was afraid of what might happen if he got too close to her right now. "I have a website. Shows a lot of my work. I'll write it down for you."

"That would be great. Thanks." She took another sip of her wine, peeking under her lashes and over her glass at him.

Was it the wine, or was she eyeing him more and more as the night went on?

"What?" he asked curiously.

Hope's cheeks flushed in embarrassment at getting caught looking at him again. "Nothing, just wondering."

His eyebrows raised as he tilted his head. "About?"

"Um, I was just wondering where you're from. I never asked." She took another big sip of her wine to try to calm her nerves.

"I was born and raised in Pennsylvania. Joined the Marines right out of high school and did two tours. I moved around a lot when I got out."

"You were a Marine?" she asked in shock.

"I am a Marine." He raised his glass to her in salute. "Once a Marine, always a Marine."

"Wow. I'm impressed. I think I may know only one other

person that's served in the military. God, that makes me sound like a snob, doesn't it?" Her cheeks flushed pink in embarrassment.

He laughed. "No, not really. I mean, I guess it depends on how and where you grew up. I live in the Village now, in Greenwich. I like the vibe in the city, and it's a great place for my work."

Hope uncurled her legs, stretching them out across the couch, almost touching his legs. He put his wine glass down on the table and absently picked up one of her feet and starting massaging it.

Her head rolled back against the couch as a loud groan escaped her lips. "Oh my God, do you know how good that feels?"

He chuckled and continued rubbing the bottom of her foot, doing magical things with his fingers. "I think I've got an idea."

"Anyway, I grew up in a small mill town, and unless you wanted to end up working at the mill, or were lucky enough to be able to get out of town to go to college, you signed up for the military. I always thought I was a tough guy, so, of course, I had to pick the Marines." He placed her foot down gently, picked up the other one, and started rubbing that one.

"Thought you were a tough guy?" she questioned between low moans of pleasure.

"Spend a few years in combat..." He was quiet for a minute, reflecting. "You find out pretty quickly that, no matter how tough you are, shitty things happen. I saw most of it from behind a lens but plenty through a scope, as well, and more than a few of my friends died."

She pulled her foot out of his hand and, leaning forward, placed her hands over his, looking him in the eyes. "I'm sorry, truly. I can't even imagine."

They stared quietly at each other for a minute. Hope ran her eyes over his features, taking him in now that he was completely dry and she was feeling a little bolder from the wine.

His hair, a medium chocolate color now that it was dry, was long, at just above his shoulders, and a bit shaggy, but it had some curl to it. He kept it brushed back away from his face, which was more rugged in nature due to the few days of scruff he sported. It caused the green of his eyes to stand out in contrast to the rest of his face. His top lip was more defined and fuller than his bottom lip, but they fit his face perfectly. He took a sip from his glass, and his tongue darted out to lick some wine off his bottom lip. She wondered if his lips were as soft as they looked. He looked up at her then and noticed she was watching him, and his mouth cocked slightly to the right in a grin.

Gage leaned forward and, pulling his hand from hers, brushed hair that had fallen forward over her face back behind her shoulders. He cupped the side of her face, swiping his thumb down her cheek and over her lips. She relished the tender feel of his hands cupping her jaw and leaned into his touch. Opening her mouth slightly, she traced his thumb with her tongue, closing her eyes at the salty taste. He moved his hand to grasp her lightly behind the head, pulling her in and sweeping his lips across hers, barely grazing them.

Hope moved closer to him and pressed her lips more firmly against his, telling him with her lips that she wanted more. He took his other hand and, reaching around her waist, pulled her even closer, never breaking contact with her mouth. She moaned in acceptance and pleasure.

She wrapped one hand around the back of his neck, running her fingers through his hair, holding it tightly, while the other grabbed the front of his t-shirt, bunching it in her fist. His tongue pushed against the seam of her lips, and she parted them for him, their kiss intensifying. Gage pulled her closer still, so she threw her leg over him as she slid against him, and his hand lowered down her back and pushed her core against his.

Hope moaned, low and guttural, as she felt his erection press against her, and instead of pulling away, rocked her hips into him. Just his kisses were making her feel more than any man had in the last five years.

Gage groaned at her rocking motions, his lips leaving hers and roving down her neck, hot and wet. Licking and then biting and sucking. She let her head fall back as she felt every nerve ending come alive, her nipples hardening, her core throbbing and wet. She had both hands wrapped around his broad back and started to pull up on the back of his t-shirt to get it off.

"Off," Hope mumbled. "I want to feel your skin."

He let go of her long enough to pull it over his head,

throwing it on the floor next to the couch. Her hands were immediately gliding over his bare back, feeling the smoothness of Gage's skin but also the strength in the muscles covering him. His lips found their way back to her neck, kissing her lower, unbuttoning her shirt, and then moving lower still until she felt him suck her taut nipple into his mouth. Hope moaned at the intense pleasure, as he licked and then bit lightly, suckling the rigid peak, causing her to jerk against his hardened length. He groaned in approval and shifted his body so Hope was positioned perfectly against his raging cock.

"Do you want me to stop?" he asked, breathing heavily. He looked up at her, his face as flushed as hers surely was.

"Don't you dare," was all she replied before slamming her mouth back to his, running her hands over his toned arms and then skimming her fingers through the light hair spattering his chest. This time, she moved her lips down his neck, slowly nipping and sucking as she trailed her tongue down his stomach. Once she reached the band of his sweatpants, she slipped off his lap and knelt on her knees in front of him. She pulled at the string holding up his sweatpants and started to push them down over his hips. He lifted his hips, allowing her to strip him naked.

She leaned back and looked at him, admiring every physical detail. Hope could see that the tattoo over his heart said Faith in beautiful cursive. A girl or a reminder to himself? When she brought her hand up and began tracing her fingertips over the tattooed script, Gage's entire body tensed up and he frowned. He took her hand lightly then and brought it to his mouth where he kissed each of her fingers, sucking the tips slowly into his mouth. She felt her body quiver as he traced his way across her palm, over her wrist, and down her arm, pulling her to him as he did. When she was close enough, Hope braced her hands on his strong shoulders as he unbuttoned the rest of her shirt and pushed it back to slide down her arms.

Gage pulled her up onto her knees and then pushed her yoga pants down over her hips. She reached for them then and pushed the pants the rest of the way down her legs as he threaded his hand through her long, golden hair and around the back of her head, pulling her mouth to his again.

Hope climbed back on him, their kiss becoming more heated. She wrapped her arms around him and pressed her flat stomach to his solid one and slid her wet core up against his cock, rocking back and forth. He groaned into her mouth, grabbed one of her pert breasts with one hand, a handful of her hair with the other, and pulled her head back before biting her neck, kissing her roughly.

He kissed his way up to her ear and whispered one last warning, "Are you sure about this?"

She thrust her hips and met his hardened length with her wet and heated entrance, sliding slowly up and down. She let out a pleasure-filled moan as her head fell back in desire. "Does it feel like I'm sure?"

"Holy shit, woman. You're going to kill me," he drawled as he pulled her head up so that he could look her in the eye.

"No, not kill you, just fuck you." She kissed him hard and, moving her hips, slid his hard cock up and into her slick core. She gasped as her body adjusted to his size, her walls clenching around him and then relaxing as she pushed down and seated herself fully on him. No more words were needed. Their bodies did the talking as they held on to each other and felt every push, pull, and slide until they both came undone. When they were finished, Hope found herself wrapped in Gage's arms on the couch. She pulled a blanket over them, and they held each other as they both fell into a contented sleep.

Chapter Four

Sunlight streamed in through the wall of glass that made up the backside of the house, brightening the living room, causing Hope to blink her eyes several times as she tried to adjust to the light. She raised her hand to shield her eyes, and that's when a warm grip tightened around her waist and pulled her into its embrace. A smile ghosted over her lips as thoughts of the night before ran through her mind, a small groan of embarrassed satisfaction escaping as she curled against the hard body behind her. *She picked a stranger up off the side of the road and ended up having mind-blowing sex with him!*

"Don't get up yet." His voice vibrated deeply against her neck, causing goosebumps to break out across her body. "I just want to feel you against me for another minute."

"Okay." She scooted herself back until her entire body was flush with his, almost purring when his arms wrapped tighter to hold her possessively. She could feel his heart beating against her back, his hot breath gently breezing through the strands of her hair. As she grazed her fingers lightly over the muscles that corded his forearms, she blushed at the memory of them grasping onto her as she rode him.

"What are you smiling about?" His voice grumbled behind her.

"How can you tell I'm smiling?" Her smile grew even wider.

"You are, right?"

"Maybe." She tried hard to stifle the giggle trying to escape.

Before she could react further, her body was flipped around and Gage was pressed down on top of her, a wicked gleam in his eyes. He leaned down and ran his tongue languidly around her ear before whispering, "I like making you smile." He continued to trail his tongue down her jawbone before making his way to her lips, tracing them lightly before nipping playfully. "And I like how swollen and pretty these look after I kiss you."

She let out a gasp of surprise as his mouth captured hers completely in a searing kiss, his tongue snaking inside, dancing together with hers. She slid her hands up over his broad shoulders and around his neck, pulling him tighter against her raging body. Her legs fell open as he pushed himself up against her core, a low growl of desire sounding in his throat. His lips tore away from hers, causing a strangled groan to escape her lips as her eyes flew open in question. He leaned his forehead against hers, his eyes capturing hers, his breathing heavy.

"I probably should have brought this up last night, but protection?"

She felt her cheeks heat in embarrassment as she realized that was something she should have thought to ask about, as well. Damn wine and his fine body had made her senseless. "I'm on the pill, so, um, I think we're okay, and I actually was just tested. I'm clean." She thought about her lying, cheating boyfriend for only an instant.

"I haven't been with anyone in about six months. I can wear a condom if you want?"

She moved her chin up and brought her mouth up to his, kissing him slowly. Not moving her mouth from his, she whispered, "The only thing I want inside of me is you. Just you."

"Thank you, Jesus," was all she heard before his lips crashed back against hers and his hands wrapped around her waist, pulling her body back to his. She arched her hips up to rub against his—

BRRRING! They both froze, their lips breaking apart. BRRING!

"That's the phone." She pushed gently against his chest and rose to sit up. "The power must be back on."

Gage moved completely off her, his eyes following her as she wrapped a blanket around her nakedness and walked to a phone on the wall next to the pantry entrance. She lifted the receiver off the cradle and brought it to her ear.

"Hello?"

"Hope dear, is that you?" Her father's concerned voice carried over the line.

"Daddy? Of course, it's me. What's wrong?" She heard a sigh come from the other end of the line.

"Dearest, I hadn't heard from you since yesterday, and you weren't answering your cell. I've been worried."

Nothing like a call from her father to throw cold water onto the flames that she was about to ignite into. "Oh, Dad, sorry about that. No power here last night because of the storm, and my cell was dead. I didn't even realize the power was back on. I was just waking up."

She watched as Gage stood up and bent down to retrieve the sweatpants that had been discarded on the floor the night before. She couldn't help but admire his ass and had to drag her eyes away in order to pay attention to her father.

"What was that, Dad?"

"I said, is everything okay up there? Should I send one of the caretakers out to check on things?"

"Oh, no, that shouldn't be necessary." She watched in disappointment as Gage pulled the t-shirt over his head and looked away quickly when his eyes caught her staring. "I'll take a walk around the property, and if I need anything, I know who to call."

"Okay, dear, just keep me posted. Please be careful up there and get some rest."

"I will, Dad. Promise. Love you."

"Love you too, Hope."

She turned to hang the phone up and smiled when she

felt a pair of strong arms wrap around her, followed by warm lips up against her cheek.

"Good morning."

She turned in his arms and rested her free hand against his chest, bringing her eyes up to meet his. "Good morning to you."

He leaned down and kissed her, his lips feathering over hers before pressing more firmly, his tongue stroking her bottom lip as he pulled away. "I guess I should call the rental company."

She felt her heart dip just a little in disappointment at the thought of him leaving and couldn't help the frown that appeared. Although she barely knew him, she was surprised at how much she wanted him to stay.

His eyebrows shot up, and his head tilted in confusion. "What? Don't call the rental company?"

"Yes, of course, you need to call them. Do you have the number? We can look it up if you need it. I'm sure there's a phone book in one of these drawers." She moved to walk around him to make herself busy looking for the phone book, but he grabbed her wrist gently and pulled it so she was facing him.

"Say it."

Her brows creased, and her eyes narrowed. "Say what?"

He took a step closer, and she could feel the pulse in her wrist increase as he did. When he licked his lips and dragged his eyes up her body, Hope stifled a low moan before meeting his eyes with her own. "Say it, Hope."

She shifted nervously and looked away, huffing out a

breath. "I'm not sure what you want me to say, Gage," she mumbled, hoping he wanted to stay as much as she wanted him to.

He leaned even closer and grazed his lips lightly over hers. "Tell me you want me to stay."

Her eyes widened, and Hope held on to her anticipation, looking up at his face again, trying to read him. "I… You must… I…"

A sly grin fell on his lips as he shook his head. "I what? I must? Is it that hard to ask me?"

Could he possibly see how badly she wanted him to stay? Flustered and not wanting to give in so easily, she told him, "I barely even know you." She desperately needed to gain back some of the ground she had lost with her earlier stutter.

"But do you want to? Because I'd really, really like to stay and get to know you better."

Unable to hold it in any longer, a smile broke across her features, her eyes lighting up. "You would?"

He nodded slowly, his eyes still locked on hers. "I would."

"But, what about your car? Don't you have a plane to catch this morning?"

He stepped forward until his body was flush with hers, his hand releasing her wrist to slide around her waist and hold in her place. Her head tilted back as she looked up at him, her eyes never leaving his.

"Flights can be rescheduled. Tow trucks can be called. I don't have anywhere I need to be until Wednesday." His voice sounded low, dark, and needy.

"Oh." Her voice was soft even to her own ears, coming out breathy and more relieved than she wanted to let on.

Gage's eyes darted to her mouth as her tongue flicked out and ran quickly over her plump bottom lip before her teeth captured just the corner in a bite. Her lip was pink and puffy against the white of her teeth, and he wanted nothing more than to replace her bite with his. Instead, he brought his free hand up to cup her face and used his thumb to pull it free. He leaned in and swiped his tongue lightly over the part of the lip she had been grasping. When he felt her suck in a quick breath at his touch, he flicked his eyes back to hers, growling lightly. "Say it."

Her response came out like an exhale, filled with enough lust and wonder and need to match his own. "I want you to stay."

"Why didn't you just say so?" His grin was instant and victorious before he covered her gasp of surprise with his lips, silencing any further questions or doubt she may have had. He felt her blanket slide down her body, knowing she'd finally released the death grip she'd had on it, and let out a satisfied groan as she wrapped her arms around his neck, deepening their kiss.

His hands trailed down her body before coming to rest on her ass. Tightening his grip, and without tearing his lips from hers, he hoisted her up onto the island behind her. She gasped as her skin hit the cold marble, giving him just enough time to yank his shirt quickly over his head before slamming his lips back on hers. Their tongues danced together in a swirl of mixed desire, their moans echoing against the kitchen walls.

He slid his lips from hers and began trailing them softly down her throat, one hand moving to cup lightly around her breast, his fingers teasing the nipple. Her head fell back, her nails grazing across his back as she arched into his touch. He hissed at her assault, sucking her peaked nipple into his mouth, eliciting a low 'Oooo'. Her nails moved from his back to grasp onto the scruff of his neck. He couldn't help the grin forming at her response to him or the raging hard-on tenting the sweats.

Reaching down with one hand, Gage pushed the pants off his waist then used his feet to push them down and out between his legs, moving his mouth off her nipple and down her taut stomach as he did. He used his other hand to gently push her back against the cold marble until she was lying flat, her body open and exposed to him. She looked up at him from under heavy lashes, lust heady in her stare. He scanned the length of her body, really seeing it for the first time, given the darkness of the night before, and marveled at its perfection.

Her long hair fell in waves, creating a yellow halo around her angelic face and kiss-swollen lips. Her perfectly rounded breasts rose and fell quickly with each excited breath she took, exposing a flat, rigid stomach. Her legs were long and lean and bent at the knee, while her feet braced on the counter, toes painted the perfect shade of pink. Her legs were open just enough to allow him a view of her pussy, which glistened with evidence of her want and need.

He ran his hand down the length of her body, stopping at her core before running his fingers through her lips, both of them groaning at the touch. He slid one finger inside her and began moving it slowly in and out, pushing her legs open wider, kissing down the inside of her thigh.

"Oh my God, yes, Gage. That feels so good." Hope mewled her approval softly, fueling Gage's desire to please as she ground her hips trying to get closer to his touch.

"You like that, Angel?" Sliding another finger inside her heat, he continued his rhythm, his mouth now hovering just over her clit. He darted his tongue out and swiped lightly at the swollen nub, her salty essence exploding on his taste buds. Her loud moan of gratification was all he needed to press his tongue flat against her core and lick heavily. Arching her back off the counter, she pushed herself up against his mouth, another song of appreciation coming from her.

"You taste so fucking good, Hope." He thrust his fingers in more deeply, strumming his tongue back and forth over her clit, her hips thrusting in time to his strokes. Gage clamped his mouth over her pussy and sucked, humming at the same time, knowing the vibrations would send her over the edge.

"Oh, my… I'm going to come if you… Oooooohhh!" Her foot slid off the counter and onto his shoulder, grinding into it as she tightened around his fingers, her pussy convulsing, her wetness met by his eager lips. He continued to pump his fingers in and out of her, but pulled his mouth away, looking up to see the bliss on her face. Standing up straight, he pulled his fingers out, grasped his cock, and lined it up so he could sink into her wet, throbbing core and…

Bang! Bang! Bang!

They both rose to attention, their eyes flying open, before turning in the direction of the noise. Gage still had his cock fisted in his hand, when the same banging sounded again, this time with a questionable greeting.

"Hope? You home? It's Walter. Your dad called and asked me to come check on you."

Gage sighed under his breath, not believing he was being cock-blocked by her dad, again. "You've got to be fucking kidding me."

Hope sat up on the counter, her cheeks turning pink, a small smile playing at the corners of her mouth. "Ssshh. I don't want him to know you're here. The first call he'll make is to my father, and that's the last thing either of us want."

She jumped down off the counter and, instead of wrapping herself back in the blanket, threw on the shirt and sweats that Gage had been wearing. He looked at her, shaking his head, a questioning look in his eyes. "And what do you want me to do?"

She pointed to the pantry, jumping a little in place, her nervousness getting the best of her. "Just go hide in there."

"Seriously?" His eyebrows raised in disbelief. As much as he didn't want to deal with her dad by being caught, he couldn't believe she was sending him to hide in the pantry.

"Please." She jumped up and kissed him quickly on the

cheek, just as Walter began banging on the door again. "I gotta get that before he barges in!" She scurried off in the direction of the front door as he reached for the blanket on the floor. Wrapping it around his waist, he shook his head and, feeling like a thief, walked into the pantry, shutting the doors behind him as he went.

Chapter Five

Fifteen long minutes later, Hope pushed the pantry door open and peeked her head in. "You still here?"

He was sitting naked and cross-legged on the blanket, his hand stuffed in a box of Froot Loops strategically placed on his lap. "You got any milk?"

She couldn't help the laugh that erupted. "Are you having a picnic? And I wasn't invited?"

"You left me for Walter. It's your own damn fault." He winked playfully at her as he stood up. "I'm starving. You think the milk is still good?"

"How about you get dressed and then we can take a ride into town to deal with your car and grab some food. I know a cute cafe we can hit up." She snaked her hand into the box and pulled out a small fist of cereal before he could close it up. Smiling, she tossed the loops into her mouth and began chewing. "You're right; we need milk."

Less than thirty minutes later, after they both took a quick shower, separately, they were back in her Range Rover and on the way into town. Though it was late September, the air was pleasantly warm. The sun sparkled through the red, golden, and green leaves, creating the most brilliant color palette nature could provide.

"I should have brought my camera," Gage murmured as he watched the blazing colors of the tree line whiz by.

"We can go out later if you want, either in the boat or I know some great spots on the back roads. I should take you to this covered bridge over off Route 2. You would love it."

He turned his gaze from the window, an easy smile gracing his face, his eyes crinkling in delight. "That would be amazing." His eyes swept down her form, appreciation apparent at her more relaxed state of dress of faded boyfriend jeans, a plain white t-shirt, and black sneakers. Quite a contrast, not only compared to the dress she'd been wearing when they met, but she knew she also felt more relaxed. Though they'd just met, Hope had felt a level of peace take hold of her overnight.

She turned her eyes away from the road and gave him a quick glance. "What are you staring at?"

His cheeks turned upward, again with those damn green eyes crinkling. "You seem more relaxed today. Happier."

She met his smile with one of her own and admitted, "I am. I love it here. The lake house is where I feel most at home."

"Why don't you live here full time then, instead of the city?"

She shrugged as she replied, "Work. I love that, too, and I need to be in the city most of the time for that."

"How often do you get to come up here then?"

"Not as much as I'd like; that's for sure." She pointed out the windshield for him to look ahead. "Look, there's the little cafe I was telling you about. It looks open!"

"Good, because I'm starving."

She laughed. "That seems to be an ongoing situation for you."

"Feed me then, woman. I am a man and need sustenance!"

They were both laughing as they rolled into the parking lot, and she slid into one of the available spots, shutting off the engine. He jumped out and made his way around to her side, pulling the door open, startling her as she gathered her purse.

"Oh!" Her eyes went from him to the door to him again. "Are you opening the door for me?"

He held out his hand to help her step out of the truck and nodded. "Don't men usually do that for you?"

She scoffed, "Only my paid driver."

An odd look appeared on his face at her statement, his eyebrows raising in question. "No one? Not an ex-boyfriend?"

Now, it was her turn to raise her eyebrows and reply dryly, "Let's not go there." That just wasn't a conversation she was comfortable having at the moment. Again, he pulled the door open for her and waited for her to enter first. She smiled appreciatively. "Looks like your momma raised you right."

They were immediately greeted by a hostess upon entering, who may have had one too many cups of coffee that morning. "Well, good morning, you two! Can I get you a table? Are you wanting breakfast with us today, and is it just you two lovebirds?"

Gage took that opening to wrap his arm around Hope's waist and pull her close to him. "Yep, just us two lovebirds this morning." He then brushed a kiss across the top of her head, and she heard his soft inhale as if he were smelling the lemony scent of her shampoo. "We've worked up quite an appetite this morning."

Hope's eyes flew wide at the same time her mouth fell open, and she turned to gawk at him. He gave her a quick wink and pulled her to follow the waitress, who was giggling behind the menus at his insinuation. She sat them at a small table by the window, handing the menus over before scurrying back to the hostess station.

"You are wicked," she hissed across the table, trying to suppress the grin threatening to break across her features.

"Being bad is so much more fun, don't you think?" He tilted his head in question, his eyes crinkling again around the corners before he lifted the menu and broke their contact.

She kept her gaze locked on him, even though she could no longer see his face. She was content to take in the way the cords of his finely muscled arms moved when he drummed his fingers across the back of the menu, or looking at the bottom half of the cross tattoo as it peeked out beneath the sleeve of his t-shirt. Well, her brother's t-shirt. She had given him a shirt to wear, but he chose to wear the jeans he had on last night, claiming they were 'mostly' dry. She was remembering how good his butt looked in those jeans when he plopped his menu flat on the table.

"You gonna order off the menu, or do you have something else in mind?" He cocked his head, a wicked grin on his face.

"Of course, I'm ordering off the menu. What else is there?" She decided to play dumb and not feed his ego, grabbing the menu out from under his hands and reading it.

"Uh-huh, whatever you say." He chuckled and sighed in relief when a waitress appeared with a pot of hot coffee and two mugs in her hand.

"Coffee?" She set the mugs down on the table as she asked.

"Yes!" They both answered in unison and reached for a mug.

"Rough night? Storm got pretty bad for a while." The waitress, whose name tag read Tilly, moved to fill both their mugs with hot, steamy, liquid caffeine.

Hope and Gage shared a quick look across the table, both smiling a bit shyly, before he responded. "Nope. Wasn't too bad at all. Pretty good, actually."

"Well, I guess you both got lucky then, huh?" Tilly pulled some creamers out of her apron and plopped them on the table between them.

Gage looked directly at Hope as he answered, his gaze dark, "Yep, I sure did."

"You two know what you'd like?" She set the coffee pot

down on the table and pulled a pen and pad out of her magical supply apron, ready to jot down their orders.

"You know what you want?" He moved his hand to gesture toward Hope. "Ladies first."

She smiled at him while shaking her head at his bravado and then turned her attention to Tilly. "I'll have the Sunrise Special, over easy, wheat toast please."

"You want any meat with that? We've got bacon, sausage, ham, or steak."

"Bacon would be great. Thanks."

Tilly turned her attention to Gage. "What about you, handsome?"

"I'll have the same, but I'll take sausage, please. And I'd like a glass of orange juice."

"You got it." Tilly turned to leave. "Be back in a jiff. Just shout if you need something."

"Thank you," they said in unison again. They shook their heads in light laughter at their repeated 'jinx' and then each took a mug of coffee. He drank his as it was, hot and black, humming in appreciation after a deep sip. She emptied in her third creamer, after putting two sugars in, before stirring and finally bringing the mug to her lips.

"Can you even taste the coffee?" he asked sarcastically.

A frown brought the curve of her lips downward. "Oh, hush up. I like a little flavor in my coffee, you big brute."

"I see that." He chuckled and took another long sip from his mug. She watched his eyes follow the trail of her gaze to the tattoo on his arm before he looked back at her, eyebrows raised. "Don't like the tattoo?"

She shook her head quickly. "No! That's not it at all.

Don't laugh, but I've actually never dated anyone that's had one before."

He chuckled at her flustered statement. "Why doesn't that surprise me? You do seem a little… uptown?"

She scrunched up her nose. "You say that like it's a bad thing. I live in the city, just like you."

"I'm sure you live in a neighborhood a lot nicer than mine, though, right?"

She shrugged her shoulders nonchalantly in response. "I like it." He looked at her curiously. "The tattoo," she clarified, pointing to his arm. "Well, tattoos. What do they mean?"

He looked down at his arm and, using his opposite hand, scrunched the material of the sleeve up so she could see the entire Celtic cross on his upper arm. "Well, in case it wasn't obvious by my name, or dark hair and green eyes, I'm Irish." He looked up at her then and waggled his eyebrows.

"That much I figured out," she responded wryly. "What about the swirly one on your other arm and chest?"

"That's a brotherhood tribal tattoo that my unit and I got after we finished our last deployment." He reached up and absently ran his hand over his other arm.

"And Faith?" She didn't know why, but she had a feeling the tattoo had nothing to do with his belief in God and everything to do with a woman, and when she saw the dark shadows sweep across his expression, she knew she was correct.

Just at that moment, Tilly arrived, breaking the tension by setting down a full plate in front of each of them. "There you go, folks. I'll be right back with your juice, handsome."

They looked at each other over the steam coming up off their plates, still silent when Tilly came back, placing the juice in front of Gage and asking if they needed anything else.

Gage shook his head. "No thanks, I think we're good. Thank you again."

She nodded her head and flitted back into action at another table next to them.

"It's okay if you don't want to tell me," she said quietly as she picked up a fork and poked at the food on her plate. "I wasn't trying to pry."

Both his hands were laid flat on the table as he looked down at his plate and then slowly up at her. "Faith was my little sister. She died six years ago. The tattoo is for her."

Hope's fork stopped midway to her mouth as a knife sliced through her heart at the pain she could hear in his voice. She knew that pain. She felt it often when she thought of her mother. Her fork met the table, and she moved her hand to place it over his.

"I'm so sorry, Gage. I had no idea. I figured an old girl-friend." She squeezed his hand, and he looked up at her, a weak smile crossing his features. "Truly, I know what it's like to lose someone you love."

He reached over with his other hand to cover hers. "Like you said last night, you think after six years it would get easier, but it doesn't." His eyes softened. "I know you weren't prying."

He released her hand and moved to pick up his fork in a signal that the conversation was over. She mimicked his move and began to eat.

The herbs in the fried potatoes exploded on her tongue, causing her to moan loudly. "Oh my God! Those are so good! Taste them."

He smiled broadly and scooped a forkful into his mouth, humming in appreciation. And just like that, the tension of the moment was forgotten.

Chapter Six

It was just after eleven when they pulled back up to the lake house. They had stopped at the car rental office to deal with that mess and also made a quick stop at the grocery store to grab some fresh items for the refrigerator. Gage hopped out and, once again, came around to open the door for her. He then scooped the grocery bags off the back seat.

Walking by the old blue pickup truck also parked in the yard, he stopped and tilted his head in its direction. "What's the story with old blue here if you have the Range Rover?"

She smiled at the truck fondly and rubbed a hand over the edge of the hood. "It was my mom's. She loved this truck. I don't have the heart to get rid of it."

"Does it still run?"

"Like a dream. Walter is a champ when it comes to upkeep on it." She patted it affectionately and then continued up onto the porch, unlocking the door and moving into the house.

They worked together to toss out the milk, creamer, ice cream, eggs, and sour cream that had been in the fridge all night, restocking it with the items they picked up in town.

"So, whatcha feel like doing?" She leaned up against the island and looked out over the lake. "Any interest in taking the boat out for a little bit? It's so nice today, and the water looks really calm."

She watched as he shifted to get a better look out the full-length windows at the lake beyond before looking back at her. "You can bring your camera. I bet you can get some great shots."

He ran a hand over his stubble and then turned his body toward hers, placing a hand on either side, effectively pinning her in. She spun around and looked up into his devilish eyes, her hands moving to rest on his chest. His heart thumped quickly at her soft touch. He bent and swept a kiss across her lips, his eyes locking onto hers.

"Sure, we can do that if you want." His eyes shifted to scan down her body, his lips brushing hers again lightly, moving as he spoke. "Or we can do this…" He pressed his lips more firmly against hers, swiping his tongue across the seam of her lips, coaxing her to open them. She complied, moaning softly, her body becoming pliant against his.

"Okay," she murmured through their kisses. "This is good, too."

Her head fell back as he placed kisses down her neck until he reached the collar of her t-shirt. He ran his tongue along the edge and then blew on her wet skin, causing goosebumps to break out across her flesh. "I've been wanting to kiss you since breakfast."

She lifted her head to meet his eyes, a sexy smile on her lips. "Do you mean kiss me, or do you mean *KISS* me?"

He grinned wickedly before responding, "I mean *KISS* you." He smashed his lips to hers again and reached down to scoop her into his arms before turning and walking toward the stairs. He made his way up slowly, continuing to kiss her, careful not to trip with her in his arms. "Which room?"

She pointed left, panting softly from their kisses. "First door on the left."

He strolled down the hall, banging the door open with his foot, and entered the room. He stopped short as his eyes took in the room. "Holy shit. This is gorgeous."

From the second floor, the view of the lake was breath-taking. He took in the large king-sized bed covered in a handmade comforter sitting adjacent to another massive fireplace. Beautiful soft rugs were scattered across the colored hardwood floors.

Hope lay forgotten in his arms for a moment as he looked around the room and noticed all the soft personal things that made it hers; a bouquet of white silk roses in a silver vase by the bed, picture frames filled with what he had to assume were her friends and family on the dresser and book case, books littering almost every free flat space in the room.

She wriggled in his arms and cleared her throat. "Um, sure, the room is nice, but remember me?"

Her melodic voice broke him out of his trance and brought his attention back to her. He smiled at her, bending to kiss her lips lightly before walking to the foot of the bed and setting her down. "Sorry."

She scooted back, her eyes burning into his as he knelt on the bed and crawled up and over her body, his knees resting between her legs. The muscles in his arms strained tightly, his tattoos dancing out from under his shirt sleeves as he lowered his lips and began kissing her. Her hands trailed up over his strong arms and tangled in his hair. He dropped to his elbows and splayed his long fingers around her head, holding her firmly in place, his mouth continuing to slay hers.

Ever so slowly, he lowered the rest of his body, moving one of his legs on the other side of hers, balancing his weight there. One hand moved to bunch the fabric of her t-shirt, pulling it up and over her head. Their kiss broke for only a second, just long enough for her to slide her hands down to yank his shirt off, too. Her hands floated across the inked portion of his upper arms before snaking behind his neck again, his mouth consuming hers.

His hand lingered at the nape of her neck, his fingers stroking her pulse point as if trying to slow down the pounding of her heart. Instead, the movement was like throwing gasoline on the flame he was igniting. He wanted to touch every inch of her. She turned her head to break the hold his mouth had on hers, soft pants escaping them both, his grip on her head tightening as he opened his eyes to question her, his brows furrowed.

"What?" He leaned his forehead against hers. "Is something wrong?"

She moved to shake her head back and forth, so he loosened his grip.

"Am I hurting you?" His eyes filled with concern.

She shook her head again, this time more freely, a whispered response falling from her lips at the same time. "No."

"What is it? Do you want me to stop?" He started to raise himself off her, but her hands reached out and gripped onto each of his forearms, pulling him back.

Her cheeks flushed in heat. He could tell she wanted to ask something but was too shy without the wine they'd shared last night. Finally, her request met his ears, soft and needy. "I want you to touch me. I want to feel your hands all over me."

She tightened the grip she had on his forearms, her nails digging into his tender flesh, pushing her body up as she pulled him down. His cock instantly hardened at the desperation in her touch. Darkness invaded, his concern disappearing as he greedily raked his eyes down her body. The muscles in his arms bunched as he pushed himself up into a kneeling position. Her nails dragged down his arms lightly with the motion, the sensation urging him on.

He took her hands and, bending over her, raised them above her head, his hands pushing down onto hers to add pressure. "Keep them there."

He tilted his head, watching for a response from her. She nodded quickly, a breathy response falling from her lips. "Okay."

His grip loosened then, his fingers grazing lazily down the length of her arms until he reached the juncture of her chest. He stretched his hands wide and moved them languidly down the outside of her tiny frame, his touch soft feeling her skin blaze hotter under his fingers. His hands continued, spanning wide across her stomach and then up and over her peaked breasts.

She moaned as his hands grazed over her hardened nipples, her eyes sliding shut. "Yes, like that, Gage."

When his hands reached her neck, she moaned, and he swept his tongue against her lips. Her hands rose involuntarily to gather him, but before she could touch him, his hand flew out and pushed hers back to the bed.

"Nope." He shook his head back and forth, his fingers grasping her chin, his lips nipping hers. "This is me touching you."

Not waiting for a response, he splayed his hand wide, dragging it down her center, his teeth following, nipping lightly where his hand had just been. She trembled under his touch, a low whimper floating from her, her hands twitching to stay locked above her head. He trailed his hands lower, reaching her feet and gently pulling her sneakers off. He ran his tongue up the arch of her foot and smiled as her body jerked in response. A gravelly chuckle rumbled from his throat as he ran his hands up the outside of her legs and then back across the span of her waist again.

He slid his tongue over her belly button and swirled around the small diamond that sat there. He flicked his tongue over it lightly and looked up at her through his lashes, growling, "I like this. Unexpected. Sexy."

He darted his tongue over it again as his fingers worked to unclasp the button and unzip her jeans. Dragging his tongue down away from the belly ring, he grazed it along the seam of her panties and pushed her jeans down. Her hips lifted off the bed as he slipped them down past her ass, pulling them off entirely.

❧

With him now standing before her, Hope locked her eyes on his. She watched his hands move to the button of his own jeans now—unclasping, unzipping, shoes toed off, material sliding down onto the floor. His erection strained against the front of the tight boxer briefs he wore, and she couldn't help the groan that escaped when he wrapped his hand over the width and adjusted it. She wanted that inside her.

"Come here," she mewled out, trying to contain the desperation she felt. "What are you waiting for?" Frustration and need laced her question.

His gaze travelled up her body and stopped at her eyes. "You're beautiful, Hope. I know you've probably been told that a hundred times, maybe a thousand. But, Jesus, you really are fucking gorgeous."

She sat up, her heart stuttering at his compliment, surprise temporarily claiming her voice. "I… Gage…"

He stalked to the side of the bed and sat down next to her. "Kiss me, Hope."

His voice was rough, needy, and full of lust. She didn't hesitate; she couldn't deny him when she wanted it just as much. As she pressed her lips to his, they both groaned in need. His hands came up and threaded tenderly through her hair as their kiss intensified. She pushed into the kiss, applying pressure to his arms, urging him onto his back. In one fluid motion, she straddled him and rubbed her core against his hard length.

He growled softly into her mouth as she released a guttural moan. She slid back and forth over him, her panties becoming soaked from the motion, her pussy wet and aching with need. Their teeth clacked together as they moved roughly, their greed for one another becoming frenzied. His hand pressed against her lower back, urging her to ride him harder. She arched, allowing her clit to rub roughly against him. His hands gripped onto her hips suddenly, holding them in place as he tore his lips from hers.

"I'm going to come right now if you move another inch." His face was flushed as a bead of sweat weaved its way slowly down his forehead toward his eye. She leaned forward and licked at the bead, the salty flavor coating her tongue. Lifting her hips slowly off his throbbing cock, she slung her leg over so she was on her knees beside him.

"Okay." A sly smile graced her mouth. "It's my turn then."

"For wh—" His question was answered when she placed both her hands wide on his chest and fanned her fingers through the hair sprinkled there.

"My turn to touch you." She leaned over and kissed him lightly before dragging her mouth over the light stubble coating his chin and neck. She ran her tongue slowly down the arc of his neck to his shoulder where the tribal tattoo started. Using her finger, she followed the path of the tattoo, her tongue chasing behind, nipping and licking as it went.

When she reached his bicep and the end of the tattoo, she lifted his hand and kissed each fingertip before placing his index finger in her mouth and sucking, her teeth grazing lightly as she pulled it out with a pop.

His cock jerked in approval at the attention she bestowed on his finger. He arched an eyebrow at Hope. "Perhaps not quite the angel I thought you were?"

She raised her eyebrows, feigning innocence, and crawled up his body, where she kissed along the other side of his neck until she reached the Celtic cross on his shoulder. Her body lay across his as she moved her finger to trace the outline of the cross, this time, her tongue licking his nipple before finally sweeping down the length of the cross. She moved back to his nipple, dragging her fingernail around its edge before moving her tongue to flick over its raised peak. His head rolled back as another low growl escaped.

A satisfied smile stretched across Hope's face as she moved to straddle him again. She stationed herself just above his jutting cock and reached around to undo the clasp of her bra, sliding the straps down her arms and dropping it to the floor. As she lowered her hands, he raised his, cupping each heavy mound and kneading softly. He positioned his fingers so that he could pinch each raised nipple simultaneously, resulting in a long *'oooh'* from Hope.

Her hips slid back as she arched into his touch, her ass grazing the top of his length. His hips flexed, and it bounced harder into her backside. She leaned forward, placing her hands flat on his chest, and lid down his body. Her breasts fell from his hands, and she raked her fingernails delicately down his abs until she reached the indent of his waist. When she looked up at him, she knew the angelic look in her eyes was long gone.

"This is the sexiest thing I have ever seen." She leaned over and ran her tongue down one of the v-sided grooves until she hit the edge of his boxers before licking back up the other side. She could feel his cock twitch under her chest as she moved, and she reveled in the pleasure she was giving him.

"We're even then, 'cause I think you're the sexiest thing I've ever seen," he growled out.

She smiled up at him as she continued to trail her tongue down the groove again, but this time, she pulled the boxers low and continued her journey south. Pulling the boxers lower still, finally freeing his cock, she quickly imprisoned it again as she slid her tongue and then her lips over him.

He grasped onto her hair and groaned loudly as her hot mouth enveloped him. "Holy shit. That feels incredible."

Her tongue swirled around the head of his cock before she sucked it back into her throat and swallowed, another long groan echoing around the room. Bobbing her head up and down, her wet mouth sliding back and forth, his grip tightened in her hair the faster she went. Her pussy was throbbing even though he was the one being touched. She could tell he was getting close by the trigger action of his hips thrusting into her mouth. She hummed around his cock, knowing the vibration would push him over the edge. Instead of the deep push she was expecting, he pulled back quickly, his cock popping out of her mouth.

She didn't even have a second to react before his arms snaked under hers, pulling her up to him, his lips locking on to hers. As she threaded her arms around his neck, meeting his passion with equal ferocity, he rolled her onto her back. His lips broke from hers as quickly as they had found them, and he moved down her body, his hands landing on her hips.

"These need to go." He grabbed onto the edge of her silk panties and pulled hard, the material cutting into her skin slightly before it finally released and tore off of her.

She yelped in shock but couldn't deny his caveman tactic caused her pussy to clench with desire. He was back on top of her in another second, his lips finding hers as he moved to position himself between her legs. She spread them wide, anxious to finally have him inside her, and she didn't have to wait. He used his hand to guide himself into her, finally slamming home in one thrust.

They moaned into each other at his welcomed intrusion and began moving as they became one. He slowed his thrusts down as he gripped her leg and bent it so he could push even deeper into her. She met him thrust for thrust, their bodies slick from sweat, slipping each time they came together. His grip on her tightened, and she knew it would leave a bruise, but she didn't care. She could feel every inch of him inside her, and it awakened a fire in her that she thought couldn't be lit again.

Her body started to tingle and tighten, and she knew her climax was close. Her eyes clenched, and she dug her finger-nails into Gage's arms, tightening her hold on him, trying to fuse herself to him as fireworks exploded behind her eyelids, words breathlessly tumbling out of her. "I'm coming… I'm coming…"

He clung to her as her pussy clenched around his cock, tightening like a vise before finally convulsing around him, and his release burst from him in hot jetted spurts. His body went rigid, his cock throbbing in time to her contractions.

A long moan left her as she loosened her hold on him and her body began to relax. "Oh. My. God. That was so, so, so, good."

His cock was still twitching inside of her, so he pulled her back against his body. "Not so fast. I'm not ready to leave the comfort of that nice, warm place my cock has found."

She reached up and slapped him playfully on the shoulder. "Gage!"

"What?" He chuckled. "It might be the best place he's ever been."

"He can come visit anytime he wants." As soon as the words were out, she slapped a hand over her mouth in embarrassed shock. "I can't believe I just said that!"

He pulled her in a little tighter, his chest rumbling with light laughter. "Nothing wrong with having a little company over from time to time."

She leaned her head back to look at him in feigned disbelief. "I'm not sure if I'd refer to him as *little*. But maybe I just haven't had enough *visitors* to know."

He looked down at her in confusion. "Wait, are you trying to tell me an unbelievable woman like you hasn't had many visitors? I would think you'd have company banging down your door." He laughed lightly. "Pardon the pun…"

"Well, good company is hard to find sometimes." She shrugged lightly. "Why? How much company have you had?"

"Uh-uh. Nope. Not going there." He shook his head.

"Well, that's not very fair," she retorted, her voice sulky.

"Let's just say I've had enough company to throw a good size party."

"Oh."

A very long, uncomfortable moment of silence settled between the two of them as she let his words sink in. She tensed and was about to get up.

"Wait," he murmured against her hair, holding her body to his. "I'm sorry if that offended you."

"You didn't offend me. Really, I was just thinking that I'm twenty-eight years old and haven't even had enough visitors to have a decent dinner party."

This time, he pushed her away from his chest and looked into her eyes. "You think that's a bad thing?"

She lifted her shoulders and frowned slightly. "Is it a good thing? I don't know. I probably work too much."

He placed a bent finger under her chin and lifted it to look her in the eyes. "Yes, it's a good thing. It means that me being here isn't something you take lightly. I like that I might fall into the *good company* category."

Her eyes softened at his words, and her embarrassment floated away, being replaced by something lighter in her heart. "Thank you, Gage."

He placed a soft kiss on top of her head as she rested it back on his chest. "Thank you, Hope."

Chapter Seven

Two hours later, Gage woke to his grumbling stomach. He could feel Hope's long hair splayed across his chest and moved to stroke it blindly, his lips curving upward at the memory of their afternoon. Her hand, which was resting on his chest, began to stroke back and forth lightly as her low humming vibrated over his heart.

"I can't believe you're hungry again." It came out slurred, followed by a little giggle as his stomach responded in kind.

"It's your fault."

"My fault?" She lifted her head and looked up at him under sleepy lashes.

"Yeah, your fault." He twisted and quickly flipped her so she was lying underneath him, looking up at him. "All this extra-curricular activity."

He gave her a cocky grin before grabbing her lip in a bite, his eyebrows rising seductively as he let go and slid his tongue over the small indentation his teeth left. "Luckily, you look delicious enough to eat."

Her tongue darted out to meet his, coaxing it to come out and play. He swooped his tongue out further, exploring her open mouth before fusing his lips around hers. She reached her arms up to grasp his nape, her awakened body surging against his. He imprisoned her, his arms locking tightly around her, his stomach grumbling loudly in protest between them.

Hope giggled through their kiss until she finally had to break away as they both laughed loudly. "Good lord, man. I better feed you before you starve to death!"

He looked down at his stomach, feigning anger. "Yep, I guess he's not going to wait."

She moved to climb out of the bed, pulling a blanket off the bottom of the bed to wrap around her body. "We can have dessert later." A sexy smile spread over her glowing face as she raised her eyebrows suggestively.

"Sounds good to me." He rose from the bed and, after finding his jeans, slid them on, sans boxers, leaving them unbuttoned as he moved toward her. He tugged her into his arms, engulfing her in a tight hug, and placed a kiss on her head before releasing her and stepping back. "Do you want to shower? I can go down and cook something for us."

She beamed up at him. "Do you know how much I love that you can cook? Because I hate it."

He couldn't resist pecking a kiss on her nose, enamored at how adorable she looked wrapped up in the soft yellow blanket, cheeks flushed, lips kiss-swollen and red. "It's the least I can do."

Stepping out of his arms, Hope asked, "Do you want to shower? I can get you some more clothes from Tommy's room if you want." He looked at her curiously, and she realized she had never actually told him her brother's name. "Tommy, my brother?"

He nodded, a look of relief washing over his face. *Had he actually just gotten a little jealous at the mention of another man?* "I'm good. I like having your smell on me." He grinned wickedly as her skin heated. "Are you in the mood for anything in particular?"

She shook her head. "Surprise me," she told him, padding toward the door leading to the bathroom.

Thirty minutes later, dressed in a pair of black leggings and a light blue flowy shirt, she swept down the stairs to find Gage in the kitchen stirring a frying pan full of vegetables and chicken, with a pot of rice boiling on another burner. "That smells scrumptious!"

The food did smell delicious, but what she really noticed was that he was still only wearing jeans. At least he had buttoned them up, but it didn't stop her eyes from sneaking another look at the trail of short, curly hair that ran right down the middle of that beautiful V between his hips. That damn V was going to do her in. She literally had to stop herself from walking over to him to trail her hands down his chiseled abs and over the grooves again.

She looked up to find him watching her, her face heating as a cocky grin spread across his face. "See something you like, Angel?"

"Sorry! I know I keep staring!" This time she didn't stop herself and walked up to him, placing her hands on his chest and running them down over his washboard stomach. When she reached the grooves, she stopped and took a quick step back, sucking a breath in. "You're just so damn perfect."

She looked up to see him looking at her with a surprised expression on his face. "Seriously. I mean, I know I haven't had many visitors, but still, this isn't something you get to see every day."

He laughed out loud at her confession. "Guess I'll keep you away from my Marine brothers then cause we all pretty much look like this. It's what happens when they make you run ten miles a day and feed you shit during deployment."

"I don't need any other Marine. I'm quite happy with you for now."

He put the wooden spoon down beside the stove and reached out to pull her back to him. She happily let herself be wrapped up in his strong arms. "Good, because I'm quite happy with you for now, too."

He stroked a thumb across her mouth before brushing his lips against hers in a chaste kiss and leaned toward her ear, brushing her damp hair over her shoulder, whispering, "You're pretty damn near perfect, too."

Her blue eyes rose up to look into his green ones, and they stared at each other in silence for a moment before he steps away reluctantly, stating huskily, "The stir-fry is going to burn."

"Yes!" She scurried around him and stood on the other side of the island. "What can I do to help?"

"I just need a couple of plates. I'll serve it right from here if that's okay with you?" He shut the burners off and grabbed a fork to fluff the rice. "Everything's ready."

She glided gracefully through the kitchen she'd grown up in to a cabinet and reached up to pull down a plate for each of them. As she turned to hand him the plates, she noticed him watching, her cheeks flushing a light pink.

"Here ya go." She handed him the plates. "Do you want something to drink?"

"I put a bottle of white in the fridge to chill a while ago. Do you feel like wine?"

She laughed. "I always feel like wine." She moved to a different cabinet and grabbed two glasses and got the wine out of the fridge.

He turned, grabbing the wine from her, and set it on the counter, popping the cork out in three twists. She held the glasses out as he poured. It was as if they had rehearsed the scene a hundred times, yet it was only the second meal they had cooked together. Hope marveled at how easy and natural things were between them.

They spent the next half hour eating casually and sharing conversation about nothing and everything. When they were full, they both worked to wash and dry the dishes, putting them all away in their place, until the kitchen was once again back in order.

"Now what?" He raised his eyebrows and grinned mischievously. "I think I remember you saying something about dessert?"

Laughing, she reached up on her tip-toes and gave him a quick peck on the lips. "Later. I really should go take a look around the property and make sure the storm didn't do any other damage last night." Her gaze strayed to the window and focused on the woods beyond.

"Okay, sure. I wasn't sure if Walter had already done that."

She shook her head. "He said, other than the downed tree along the driveway, he didn't notice anything, but I should probably look."

"I'll come with you. You never know when you're going to need a big, strong man around again." He gave her a cocky grin, puffed up his chest, and pointed at his stomach. "Especially one with abs like this!"

She slapped her hand to her forehead, groaning. "I'm never going to live that down, am I?"

He chuckled. "Not if I can help it." He ran a hand down his stomach and gave her a sexy smile. "I should probably wear a shirt out in the wild, however. Wouldn't want to tempt anyone else we might run into."

"Yeah, yeah, yeah." She turned and started walking toward the stairs. "Let me grab you something long-sleeved from Tommy's room. I'm sure it's getting cooler now."

"Perfect, thanks." He followed behind her but turned before the stairs. "Can you grab my shoes up there, too, please? I'm going to get one of my cameras to bring out with us."

"You got it," she called back as she climbed the stairs.

Fifteen minutes later, they were outside walking around the perimeter of the house, checking for any loose wires or downed limbs. After completing a full circle and finding everything in order, she suggested they head down to the lake and check on the dock and boats.

"You have boats? As in more than one?" he asked in surprise.

"No. I mean, yes, but not really." As they approached the lake, she pointed to a larger boat that was suspended in a lift next to the dock. "That's the only real motor boat we have, but Tommy's the only one who ever uses it." Then she pointed to a sailboat that was moored to the long dock and smiled wide. "That's mine. It's a twenty-six-foot Fantail. It has a small electrical motor, but I only use that to get it in and out of the dock. We also have a canoe and some kayaks."

He looked at her, his brows raised. "Seriously? You have your own sailboat?"

She shrugged. "It's a big lake. My dad gave it to me a few years ago as a birthday present."

"Ah, yes, that's right." A bit of an edge seemed to creep into his voice. "I forgot you're a daddy's girl."

She stopped short and turned to him. "What is that supposed to mean?"

His hand swept out to the sailboat. "You know, a hundred-thousand-dollar truck sitting in your driveway, and what, a fifty-thousand-dollar sailboat on your dock, both courtesy of daddy. Just says something."

"Says what?" Hope's hands hit her hips, and her chin jutted out in defiance. She wasn't going to tell him it was actually an eighty-thousand-dollar sailboat.

Gage shook his head, obviously realizing he was being an asshole, and took a step closer to her. Cupping her cheek, he blew out a long breath. "It says that you have a father who must love you very much. Sorry if I over-stepped."

She glared at him, her lips scrunched up tight, her mind in overdrive. He slid his thumb down her cheek and over her lips, then leaned in slowly, tentatively feathering his lips over hers. She relaxed a fraction, but a frown still marred her usual smile. He brushed another soft kiss against her lips, this time leaning his forehead against hers. "Seriously, Hope, I'm sorry. It's my own stupid shit and has nothing to do with you."

She pulled back from his hold and stomped her foot, crossing her arms at the same time. "I'll have you know I work really hard. Everything isn't handed to me on a silver platter."

He chuckled even though she was trying to be stern, finally nodding his head in compliance. "I'm sure you work very hard."

"Then why are you laughing at me!" She stomped her little foot again.

"Because you look so goddamn cute when you're angry." He smiled wide, and she gasped when he tugged her rigid form up against his, wrapping his arms around her in a hug. "Come here, you feisty little thing."

She looked up at him, trying unsuccessfully to suppress the smile that was trying to break free as she growled out, "You haven't even seen feisty yet, Mister!"

"Oh, this is quite feisty enough, thank you very much!" He bent and kissed her. She quickly let her smile fall back in place and could feel the surge of relief as it washed through him. "So, you sail?"

"Yeah, I sail," she replied sardonically. "Come on. I'll show her to you." She started walking toward the dock again and motioned for him to follow.

He slipped his camera off his shoulder, removing the lens cap, and turned it on as he walked. Hope was standing on the dock, the sun streaming around her as she looked out over the lake. He snapped a few shots without even thinking, capturing her serene beauty. She turned to him, and he caught each change in her expression as he continued clicking.

"Oh my God! Gage, stop!" She threw her hand up to block her face, cheeks flaming red at the attention. "I'm so not one of your models!"

He lowered the camera away from his face to stare at her in dismay. "First of all, you're more stunning than any model I've ever shot. And you better get used to getting your picture taken if you're hanging out with me. I tend to have a camera in my hand most of the time."

"Yuck! I hate getting my photo taken. I always look awful!" She shook her head in disgust.

"I find that hard to believe, but here." He walked up to stand beside her on the dock. "Look at these." He held the camera up and clicked a button to bring the last picture he took of her up on the viewer. "See? Stunning."

He watched as she absorbed the picture and turned to

look at him wide-eyed. "How did you do that? I look… well, I actually look pretty damn cute in that picture!"

"Because I'm amazing." He laughed as she rolled her eyes at his response. "No, really. You can ask anyone. I am. I'm amazing. It wasn't easy to capture your ugly mug and make it look this good."

Her eyes grew wide, and she reached out and slapped him playfully on the arm. "Oh, you are just awful, aren't you?"

"Oh, I think you know by now just how awful I am." He winked playfully at her and walked to go stand next to the sailboat. "So, this is your baby, huh?"

She moved to stand next to him and nodded her head. "Yep. She's got some great lines. It's getting too late to take her out now, though, but maybe tomorrow."

"I would love to do that." He looked over at her, screwing his face up in mock-embarrassment. "Now, it's your turn not to laugh, but I've actually never been sailing before."

"Wait, what?" She stared at him in astonishment. "But you're a Marine!"

"Yeah, I mean, I've been on boats, all kinds of them, but never a sailboat. Don't forget, I grew up in land-locked Pennsylvania!"

"Oh, then we are most definitely going out while you're here. You are going to love it. Once you feel the power of the wind, you'll be hooked."

"It's a deal. I'd love to go out." He looked over at the small sandy beach beyond the dock and nodded at the canoe resting on the grass where it met the sand. "Wanna take that out for a little while instead?"

She smiled and nodded her head. "Absolutely!" She turned and looked back toward the house. "I think the oars are under the deck. I'll go up and grab them if you want to get the canoe in the water."

"You got it." He paused and looked down at his camera. "Are you going to flip me, or is it safe to bring this with us?"

"I'm not going to flip us! No way, no how am I going in that water!" She shook her head firmly. "You can definitely bring the camera."

"Awesome." He smiled and started toward the canoe as she made her way up to the deck. He set the camera down on a tree stump before moving to flip the canoe and drag it to the water's edge. She was back in another minute carrying the oars and two life preservers.

"Do we need those?" He pointed at the orange vests. "I can swim."

"Yeah, me too, but you need one for each person in the boat." She walked up and set one on the seat of the canoe and smiled at him. "You have a nice cushion to sit on now."

He shook his head, chuckling low before grabbing the camera and slinging it around his neck. "Hop in. I'll push us out."

She did as he requested, placing an oar at the back of the canoe for him as she stepped in and made her way up to the front bench and sat down. She gripped onto each side of the canoe to brace herself as he began pushing the canoe into the water and then stepped in.

"And we're off!" he called cheerfully as he sat down, the canoe rocking slightly, as he used his oar to push them completely off the shore.

Chapter Eight

The lake was unusually calm, the water as smooth as glass until their paddles broke the surface, causing ripples to flow out around them. Every now and then, he would stop rowing and raise his camera to catch an image that caught his eye, but otherwise, they were both quiet.

She turned and looked at him. "Do you want to see something?"

He nodded his head. "Sure."

"Head toward that little island over there." She pointed to a small mound of land covered in small trees, jutting from the water.

He changed the angle of the oar to turn the canoe in the direction she pointed, both paddling in sync until they were about a hundred yards from the island.

Hope pulled her oar out of the water, twisted around in

her seat until she was facing him, and spoke in a hushed voice. "Have you ever seen any loons?"

"I'll assume you're referring to the bird." He laughed softly. "But, no, I don't think I actually have. At least, not that I remember."

"Well, there's a mommy and daddy loon that live on this island. I saw them with two babies this summer. I haven't been up since July, though, so hopefully they are still alive."

"Why wouldn't they be?" He brought the camera up and began scanning the island through his lens.

She shrugged. "Snapping turtles, speed boats, dumb people. Sometimes, the environment just isn't safe for little ones."

"Do you think we'll see them?" He continued scanning the island with his camera.

As if his request was heard on the wind, a short and then longer whistling sound carried out over the water several times. They both turned their head toward the sound, and moments later, saw three loons appear from around the island.

"Look!" She pointed in excitement. "There they are! Do you see them Gage?"

He smiled at her excitement over the pretty birds. "I see them." He brought his camera up and started taking pictures of the small feathered family as they floated closer to each other.

"Look how cute the baby is," she cooed. "Well, I guess it's not a baby anymore, and I guess one of the babies didn't make it."

Sadness crept into her voice, and he couldn't help but

turn the camera on her and capture the way every emotion reflected in her eyes and face.

"Do they mate for life?" he asked as he continued to snap pictures of everything around them.

"They used to think so, but new research says no. The birds will actually replace their mate if they don't produce babies for them or fly back to their nest in the spring."

The loons had swum past them in a wide berth and were circling back toward the island now, whistling calls to each other as they went.

"You're kidding me? They actually get divorced?" He chuckled in disbelief that some traditions carried over no matter what the species.

She laughed back. "I guess so. Who would have thought?" She looked away from the birds then and over at him. She tilted her head in curiosity as she looked at him. "Have you ever been married?"

Instead of answering her question, he asked one of his own. "Have you?"

She shook her head. "God, no."

He laughed. "You say that like it's a bad thing! Marriage not your thing?"

She shook her head again. "No, it's not that. I'd love to get married one day. I just haven't had the best luck yet with men. Ya know?"

"You?" He scanned her from head to toe. "What guy would be dumb enough to let you slip through his fingers? You're the whole package—beauty and brains."

She scoffed. "Well, the last guy I was dating, for over two years mind you, thought so highly of me that he decided screwing someone else while I was on a business trip would be a good idea. Until I came home early and caught him, of course."

"Shit. Seriously?" He frowned. "I'm sorry, Hope, but if that guy didn't know what he had, you're better off without him."

She sighed. "I guess." She looked over at him. "That's why I'm up here, actually. It just happened a few weeks ago. I needed to get away and reboot."

"Uh-oh."

"What?" Alarm crossed her features.

"Guess that makes me the rebound guy." He laughed lightly.

"Oh, no! Is that what you are? I thought I was just using you for sex for the weekend…" Her eyes danced with laughter, her cheeks turning pink at her own admission.

"It's okay, Hope." He looked down and then back up at her, all the laughter gone from his eyes, before speaking quietly. "I don't mind being your rebound guy. I'll be whatever you need me to be."

She was speechless for several minutes, absorbing his words and what they meant before responding, her heart hammering in her chest at the realization that she was starting to feel something for him. "You are exactly what I needed, Gage. Exactly. The best visitor I've ever had and the only one in a long, long time I've wanted to stay."

He smiled then, wide and open, the corners around his green eyes crinkling. "I'll stay as long as you want."

Their eyes locked, and an unspoken understanding about what might be happening between them swept over the moment. He finally broke their connection by looking up at the sky.

"The sun's going to be setting soon. We should start heading back." He moved to put the camera back around his neck and reached for his oar.

"You never answered my question," she remembered out loud.

"What question?"

"Have you ever been married?" She found that she really wanted, no, needed to know the answer.

He looked her in the eye again, a serious expression on his face. "Nope. When I mate, it'll be for life."

"Isn't that what we all wish for?"

"Wishing has nothing to do with it." He started rowing even though she was still turned toward him. "I believe, when you make a commitment to someone, one as big as marriage, it's done knowing it will be forever. For better or worse, in sickness and in health, for richer or poorer. Not just for however long you feel like it. Forever."

Her eyebrows shot up as her mouth shifted in surprise. "Not very many people believe in forever anymore."

"I do. I think, when you find the right person, forever won't be long enough." His gaze locked onto hers, his green eyes burning with intensity.

Hope shivered. Whether it be from the surge of blood racing to her heart, or from the chill starting to claim the air, she couldn't be sure, but she broke their connection by spinning around in her seat and grabbing her oar.

Attempting to lighten the conversation, she tried joking as she started rowing. "Have I ended up with the last true romantic?"

Sensing things had turned a little too serious, he joked back. "Nah, don't worry. I'm just visiting."

Thirty minutes later, with the sun starting to set in the west, the canoe slid back onto the beach. Gage jumped out and pushed the boat further up in the sand and then put his hand out to help her out of the canoe.

When her skin met his, an electrical current charged through her as if lightning had struck, sparking a flame of desire within her. Her eyes flew up to his and were met with a dark, hungry look on his face.

His hand drifted to behind her neck, seizing on, pulling her to him possessively, and he crushed his lips to hers. She clutched onto his shirt, the heat of his kiss melting her body into his. His hand on her neck kept her lips fused to his as their tongues dueled fiercely, their heated breaths mixing and becoming one. They were both moaning and grinding their bodies into each other, desire erasing reasoned thoughts.

He dropped his hands to her waist and lifted her up, urging her to wrap her legs around him as he started walking toward the dock. Reaching its edge, he placed her down and moved his hands to the waist of her jeans and began working the button. Her hands flew to his and began frantically mimicking his actions. Their breaths came out in pants of desperation as they each yanked off their pants, kicking their shoes off so they could remove them completely. Not a single word was said, but one look between them spoke volumes.

As soon as Hope's pants were free, he hoisted her back onto the dock and, moving between her legs, lined his hard cock up to her core, pushing into her in one hard thrust. Her hips surged forward into his, burying his cock completely in her heat. A deep groan rumbled from Gage as his balls bottomed out against her ass as he pushed deeper.

She mewled her pleasure, grabbing onto his ass, urging him to rock back and forth against her. This felt more desperate than the other times they'd had sex. It was like a reminder to them both that this was supposed to be a weekend of fooling around and not one where they started to fall for one another.

"Yes! Like that, Gage." She pushed into him forcefully. "Harder! Let me feel you!"

He plunged his throbbing cock as hard and deep as he could, slamming into her body with force, and she could feel him tense as his own body starting to climb toward release. Hope's body began to tighten around him, and her eyes fluttered shut as her climax claimed her.

"I'm going to come, Hope," he grunted out between thrusts.

"Yes! Yes! Come! I'm coming, too!" And then they both exploded, clutching each other tightly as her body convulsed again and again around his cock as he released inside of her, his hot seed seeping around them as the sun sank in the horizon.

Chapter Nine

"Will you pass me the shampoo?" A content smile graced her lips as warm water ran over her back, his arms wrapped around her. They'd come in from the dock and straight into the shower.

He shook his head, placing a soft kiss to her lips. "If you think you're finally done with me, I'll wash your hair."

She kissed him back and giggled. "Hey, you're the one that started things in the shower. I was minding my own business 'til you showed up."

He grinned at her wickedly. "Is that a complaint?"

He pecked her lips one final time and spun her around as he grabbed the shampoo off the counter. He poured some in his hand, inhaling the lemony fragrance that drifted in the steam as he began massaging it through her long locks.

She moaned her approval at his skilled fingers. "That feels so good."

"Hmmm. I seem to hear that a lot from you." He chuckled.

"You are pretty good with your hands." She laughed lightly, humming in satisfaction as he continued rubbing her head.

When he was done with her hair, he piled it on top of her head and squirted some soap into his hand. He moved over the rest of her body, leaving a trail of suds as he gently washed each part of her. She watched under hooded lids as he treated her body to this luxurious care and adoration. She couldn't remember the last time her body and soul had felt so at ease.

He finished and moved her under the water and again began massaging her hair and then her body until all the soap was rinsed away. "There you go. Clean as a whistle." He placed a kiss on her shoulder and moved to stand under the water with her.

"Thank you, Mr. Clean. I feel like a new woman."

"Good. Why don't you go dry off and put something comfy on?"

She looked up at him through wet lashes and shook her head. "You think I'm giving up a chance to run my hands over those super-sexy abs? No way! It's my turn."

He threw his head back in laughter. "You and these abs! They're just muscles, you know?"

She cocked her head at him, eyebrows arched, as she poured soap into her hand. "These are so much more than just muscles. These are planes of deliciousness that deserve to be worshipped. And I volunteer."

A low chuckle rumbled through his chest as she ran her hands over him, bubbles foaming under her fingers as she worked. "They are all yours, Angel, especially if they make you smile like that."

She beamed up at him, her face flushed from the heat of their passion. "I like when you call me Angel."

"You rescued me from a night on the side of the road and seem to have delivered me to heaven's gates. Definitely an angel."

He kissed her lazily, backing into the water as he did, rinsing himself off as droplets slid down over both of them. When he was clean, he broke away and turned to shut the water off. "Let's dry off."

They both stepped out of the shower, taking towels off the rack and drying off. "If you go in Tommy's room, you can wear anything in there you want. It's the door down the hall on the left."

"Okay, thanks." He wrapped the towel snuggly around his waist, tucking the end into the middle. "Stop ogling, woman, and get dressed!"

Hope jolted and covered her eyes at being called out, yet again, for staring at his magnificent stomach, before turning and skittering out the door to her bedroom. "I'm going! I'm going!"

Several moments later, they met in the hallway, both dressed comfortably—he in sweats and a t-shirt, and she in a thigh-length night shirt, with white, wooly socks on her feet. He took her hand as they started down the stairs together. She turned and looked at him in thought.

"Do you think it's weird that we've only known each

other for twenty-four hours? I mean, doesn't it seem like we've known each other for so much longer?"

He nodded. "Yeah. I'll admit, it's a bit strange. But you're right. This feels so easy."

"Easy is a good word. Or natural. I have been more myself with you than I think I've ever been with anyone." They had reached the kitchen and stopped in front of the center counter. She grinned broadly. "I'm going to guess you're hungry again?"

"See how well you know me already?" He grinned back at her. "Let's do something easy, though. Maybe some cheese, crackers, and fruit? I can start a fire, and we can relax and eat over there?" He nodded his head in the direction of the fireplace.

"That sounds divine. You start the fire and I'll get the food together?"

He nodded his head. "Perfect."

Gage headed over to the fire place and started building the makings of a fire, while she made her way to the fridge and started taking things out for their light meal.

"So, what did you mean when you said that you've been more yourself with me than anyone else? Why's that?" He was bent down on one knee as he placed kindling over paper in the fireplace.

"I don't know." She frowned and leaned against the island. "I guess because I work at one of my father's companies. Daddy's little girl, everything handed to me on a silver platter, and all those preconceived notions that go along with that."

"Not Daddy's little girl?" he asked with a cocky smile.

She threw him a playful glare as she started slicing a block of cheese. "Ha-ha. No. I mean, obviously, my dad loves me and wants to take care of me. I'm his only daughter, and my mom is gone now. But I've worked really hard to be in the position I'm in. I went to college for six years and worked during the last three years of that."

The fire was starting to crackle now, so he laid a few medium size logs over the lit kindle and placed the large screen over the opening. He made his way back over to her.

"And what is it that you do exactly? I don't think you've actually told me."

Her eyes crinkled, and her brow furrowed in thought as she tried to remember whether or not she had told him what she did. "Huh. I guess I didn't even realize. I'm the senior VP at a publishing house. I handle all the U.S. publications."

His jaw went slack and his eyes wide. "Wow. That's impressive."

She shrugged as her face turned a light shade of pink. "Yeah, I guess it is. I knew from a really young age that it's what I wanted to do, so I worked hard to get there."

"What do you publish?" He plucked a piece of cheese off the cutting board as she sliced some apples.

"Books mostly. Some periodicals. We published over ten thousand books last year."

He swept his hand around the room. "Well, that explains all the books everywhere."

She laughed. "Yeah, we read a lot around here. In fact, I should have been reading today, but someone has kept me very distracted!"

"I can take off tomorrow if you want," he responded matter-of-factly.

She was surprised when she felt her heart drop into her stomach. She didn't want that at all. Hope liked having him here with her. But, he seemed ready to leave without any hesitation, so instead of admitting she wanted him to stay, she played it cool.

"Do you want to leave? It's totally up to you. I'm fine either way." Instead of looking at him to gauge his response, she picked up the wooden board she had prepared their smorgasbord on and started walking to the living room.

Gage scratched his chin, not sure how he was supposed to respond. One second, she seemed to want him here, and then the next, it seemed like she was casually dismissing him. *Why were women always so damn complicated?* He watched as she placed the food on the coffee table and started fidgeting with everything else on the table.

Was she nervous? This was the first time since being with her that he'd seen her act twitchy like this. He walked back into the living room so he could confront her up close to see if he could figure out what was really going on in that mind of hers.

"Hope, I'll---"

"Oh! I forgot the wine," she interrupted him, jumping up and hurrying past him into the kitchen. She pulled a bottle of white wine out of the fridge and then two glasses out of a cabinet.

He stood by the fireplace and watched as she scurried back over to the table and placed the wine down. "I'll do—"

"Shit!" She spun and darted back into the kitchen again. "I forgot the cork screw."

He shook his head, a smirk sliding over his lips. Damn woman was so afraid he was going to say he wanted to leave that she wasn't going to let him say anything. Just like this morning. When she returned to the coffee table, and finally seemed to stand still for more than thirty seconds, he cautiously approached her. He took the wine bottle and corkscrew from her hands and placed them on the table. She kept her gaze focused on the table instead of on him.

"Hope." He reached out and curled a knuckle under her chin, pushing up. "Look at me."

Her head came up slowly, her gaze reluctantly locking onto his, her teeth brutally clutching onto her lower lip. He reached up and pulled it from her teeth, swiping the pad of his thumb across the imprints her teeth left, before lowering his hand and placing it on her waist.

"I want to stay." His nerves tingled in satisfaction when her eyes brightened before him. "Just for the record. But, if you need to work, I can go."

She peered up at him through her dark lashes, her pouty lips turning upward. "So, you don't want to go?"

He shook his head as a delightful smile lit up his face. "No." He leaned down and kissed her tenderly. "Don't want to go."

A smile illuminated her face. "Good, because I don't

want you to go. Work can wait." She stretched up on tip-toes and brought her lips to his in a triumphant kiss, arms wrapping around his neck to follow it up with a hug. His arms snaked around her waist, pulling her so close he could feel the beat of her heart against his, dazed and confused at how perfect it felt.

Chapter Ten

Hope woke slowly, a Cheshire-cat smile breaking across her face as she remembered the perfect evening she shared with Gage the night before. They had sat in front of the fire for hours, talking and laughing, before finally coming up to bed around midnight. She blushed crimson recalling the hour they spent after they came upstairs, him worshipping every inch of her, before finally succumbing to exhaustion and sleep.

She turned to look at him, still sleeping peacefully next to her. The blankets were gathered at his waist, exposing his lovely chest for her viewing pleasure. Her fingers twitched to run through the dusting of hair on his chest and explore every smooth groove that turned his stomach into a work of chiseled art, but she wanted to let him sleep.

Sighing dreamily, she slid silently out of the covers and tip-toed out of the room, quietly shutting the door behind her. After a quick stop in the bathroom, she stole down the stairs into the main house. She did a clean-up of their dishes from the evening before, took a quiche out of the freezer, and popped it in the oven. After starting some coffee, she added some sausage links to a frying pan to cook, as well. She smiled, knowing food would be waiting for him and his bottomless pit of a stomach when he woke up.

While the food was cooking, she retrieved her computer bag from the entryway and brought it out into the kitchen. She took her laptop out and, while it was powering up, turned the sausages and made herself a cup of coffee.

Hope sat down in front of the computer and opened up her email frowning. Two days and almost two hundred emails sat waiting in her inbox. She clicked it shut and decided it could wait another day. She was taking a few days off, after all. Besides, what she really wanted to do is see if she could find anything out about Gage.

Opening Google, she typed 'Gage Flynn, Pennsylvania' in the search field and hit enter. In a matter of moments, the search engine returned several pages of findings. Before she could click on anything, the timer on the oven went off for the quiche. She got up and turned the oven off then turned the burner off under the sausages, as well, covering the pan to keep them warm.

After refilling her coffee, she moved to sit back at the computer again. She browsed the information that was returned and clicked on the link for a GF Photography website. His name was listed in the subtitle information, so she assumed this must be related to his work.

Bingo. As soon as the page came up, there was a page header announcing Gage Flynn Photography and links to his work. She clicked through them and found herself spellbound by his work. He had a whole gallery dedicated to pictures he took while deployed, documenting a side of the war she had never seen on television and knew would leave her haunted. He truly had a gift for capturing images and emotions in photos.

When she had viewed almost every gallery, she clicked back to the Google search page to see what other information she might find on him. Yes, she was snooping. She knew, if she asked him anything, he'd most likely answer as he seemed to be an open book, but sometimes Google was hard to resist. She scrolled down the page and froze when she caught the headline on one of the returned links: Obituary: Faith Julia Flynn, February 23, 2010.

Of course, she had to click. She wanted to know what happened. I mean, wouldn't anyone be curious about that? The full obituary came up, and she started to read.

Faith Julia Flynn, 21, died on February 23, 2010. She was born June 15, 1988, in Millvale, Pennsylvania, the daughter of Camden and Rebecca Flynn. She attended Millvale schools and graduated from Millvale High School in 2006, where she was a member of the student council, the cheer squad, and the art club. She was currently attending Pratt Institute of Art, in Brooklyn, New York, on a full scholarship.

Faith is survived by her parents, Camden and Rebecca of Millville, and her older brother Gage Michael, currently enlisted in the United Stated Marine Corps.

She also leaves her maternal grandparents, Connor and Sarah Sullivan, also of Millvale; and her paternal grandparents, Kelly and Briana Flynn of Adare, Ireland. She is also survived by several aunts, uncles, and cousins.

Funeral arrangements are being handled by the Conroy Funeral Home in Millvale. Calling hours will be Friday the 25th from 4pm to 7pm. The funeral will be private. In lieu of flowers, the family asks that you consider donations to the Millvale High School Art program.

Reading the obituary twice to see if she could discover more than what was said in the simple notice did no good. No cause of death was listed. What did that mean? Usually, that meant suicide or some kind of accidental death. No wonder Gage was reluctant to talk about his sister.

She was about to do a Google search on Faith but turned when she heard a creak on the stairs and saw Gage making his way downward. She quickly shut the screen on the laptop and got up to greet him.

"Good morning, sleepy head." He was only wearing a pair of sweats, his bare torso teasing her once again, making it exceptionally easy for her to slide her arms around his waist and pull herself flush to him.

"Good morning to you." He leaned down and placed a soft kiss on her forehead. "How can you look this beautiful at 8:30 in the morning? And do I smell food? Did you actually cook something?"

Pushing away and playfully swatting him on one of his luscious pecs, she retorted, "I can cook. I just prefer to let you do it all."

"Uh-huh. Whatever you say, Angel." He grinned at her mischievously. "What did you make me, chef?"

Hope walked around the island to the stove and lifted the lid on the frying pan. She waved her hand over the pan. "We have sausage and…" She grabbed the pot holder from the counter with one hand, opening the oven door with the other, and pulled out the hot pie tin. "Mushroom and cheese quiche!"

He groaned at the deliciousness in front of him. "Woman, you keep this up and I'll have to marry you."

Rearing back in surprise, the quiche slipped from her grip and clattered onto the stove top. "Shit!" She reached down to stop the pan from sliding off the stove, forgetting it just came out of the oven, and burnt the tops of her fingers as she made contact. "Ouch! Double shit!"

He sprinted around the island and took her fingers gently in his hand. Bringing them up to his lips, he slowly inserted one tip into his mouth at a time before blowing cool air over each wet digit, easing the burning she felt.

"Better?" Concerned eyes met her panicked ones as she slid her fingers from his grasp and nodded her head.

"Yes, thank you." She turned to walk away, but he snaked a hand around her waist and held her in place.

"What was that all about?" He tilted his head toward the stove top.

Blowing on her fingertips, she looked up at him shyly.

"What? Nothing. I lost my grip on the pan. Do you want to eat?"

He shook his head, a sly, knowing grin working its way across his mouth. "It's just an expression, Hope. A figure of speech." He placed a curled knuckle under her chin and lifted, forcing her to look him in the eye. "I promise, that wasn't a proposal for marriage."

Her brow furrowed, internally smarting that he was so sure that he didn't want to marry her, yet externally, she knew she should be relieved. "I know that."

"Uh-huh." He bent and placed a kiss on her forehead. "Good. Let's eat then."

She closed her eyes and inhaled deeply, the spicy scent of him invading her senses.

"Besides, I always wait at least five days before I ask a girl to marry me." He chuckled as he watched her eyes fly open wide and ducked when she moved to throw a pot holder at him.

"You are such a jerk!" She stomped her foot when her soft artillery missed its target.

He waggled his eyebrows. "Maybe, but how many jerks do you know that have abs like this?" He looked down and pointed at his stomach.

She laughed and smiled broadly. "You. Just you." She walked up to him and ran her hands over his stomach and then around his waist to pull him into a hug. She turned her head and placed a kiss on his chest, right above his heart where the Faith tattoo sat, reminding her of the obituary she read moments ago. A wave a sadness washed over her, causing her to squeeze him just a little tighter.

He placed a kiss on top of her head as he wrapped his arms around her. "You okay?"

She pulled back and gave him a smile. "Yep. Let's eat."

They worked together to set the table and move the food and coffee over, as well. When they were seated and had begun eating, she asked what he wanted to do for the day. It was another gorgeous day; the sky was crisp blue, the sun reflecting off the waves of the lake.

"I know you mentioned sailing yesterday, but I remember you saying something about a covered bridge? I'd love to get some pictures of that. I bet it's beautiful with the foliage."

She smiled brightly and nodded her head. "Sure! There was one bridge in particular I was thinking about, but there are several around here. We can spend the day driving around doing a covered bridge tour if you want?"

"That sounds great, especially with you as my guide." He gave her a wink, his green eyes twinkling with delight.

She got up and started walking into the kitchen. "Let me grab my phone and check the weather to see if this is supposed to last all day."

She walked back to him, phone in hand, as she searched the weather site. Her brow furrowed as she read the report, a frown marring her face. "Hmm, today is going to be great. In the high seventies and sunny, but it looks like thunderstorms are rolling back in tomorrow morning."

He shrugged casually. "That's good then, right? All clear for today."

"Well, when were you thinking of leaving?" She put her hand up to indicate she wasn't finished when she noted the look of concern on his face. "Not that I'm trying to get rid of you!" She walked over and placed a soft kiss on his lips. "Not trying to get rid of you at all."

He yanked her down onto his lap, earning a surprised yelp from her as he did. "Good, 'cause I like being here with you."

She was surprised to realize that she was very happy being with him, as well, and smiled in relief that he felt the same way. "It's just that you said something about needing to be back by Wednesday."

He had begun trailing small kisses on her neck as she was talking and didn't pull away as he answered. "Uh-huh, and it's only Sunday."

"Mmm, that feels nice." She was momentarily distracted by his warm lips and pulled his head up so she could kiss him again. After a moment, she pulled her head away. "Listen for one second. Okay?"

His eyes were on her mouth, his tongue slipping out to slide across his bottom lip in hunger as he nodded his head. "I'm listening."

"I was thinking we could drive back tomorrow, but if you want to stay until Tuesday, we can take the jet, getting you home in time for Wednesday."

His brows raised up in surprise, all thoughts of kissing her vanishing. "Wait. You have a fucking jet? Exactly how rich are you?"

Her shoulders rose a fraction as a small grimace fell on her lips. "I don't know. Rich. It's the company jet. Does it matter?" No way was she going to tell him that it was her father's plane. Every time she brought up her father buying something for her, he got weird.

"You get that I'm just a regular guy, right? I joined the military because we didn't have enough money for me to go to college, and I used the skills I learned there to become a photographer. I'm not Ansel Adams."

She pushed off his lap to stand up and look down at him, her face pinched in anger. "Does it seem like I care about how much money you may or may not have?"

He shook his head, his lips forming a tight line, his eyes turning a bit darker. "No, you don't. But we aren't exactly living in the real world right now, so I want to make sure you realize who I really am."

"And you think how much money you may or may not have defines who you really are?" She could feel her cheeks heating as her anger began to boil at the surface. "Or that it defines what kind of person I am?"

He was quiet for a moment and then shook his head, his frown back. "No, you seem to be an exception to the rule."

This time, she shook her head and stomped her foot, as well. "Listen, you! I'm not sure what your hang up with money is, but get over it when it comes to me. I like you because you picked me up when my shoes were sinking in the mud, pulled a tree out of the road in a raging storm and still smiled about it, and because you started a fire for me when it was cold. You cooked for us and can kiss like nobody's business! I couldn't give a shit how much money you have."

"But will you feel that way when we're back in the real

world? When you invite me to dinner with your family and I show up on my motorcycle, wearing jeans?"

She turned to him, her eyes narrowing. "You have a motorcycle?" Then shook her head in disbelief, muttering, "Damn, could you be any sexier?"

He smirked and then stood and walked over to her. He grasped her head gently, turning it up so he could look her in the eye. "I want to believe so badly that everything will be as easy for us when we get back to reality, but my gut tells me that it won't be. We come from two completely different worlds, Angel."

She pursed her lips in frustration as her brows furrowed. "Why are you worrying about something that hasn't even happened yet? If you're so sure that we're wrong for each other, why are you still here?"

His gaze became even more intense as his expression changed, his smile and the crinkles that normally lit up the corners of his eyes both vanishing. "Isn't it obvious, Hope?"

She raised her eyes up to meet his, uncertain about what he was saying, and stammered out, "I guess not."

"You are so goddamn stubborn." He bent down then and smashed his lips over hers in a searing kiss, his hands still clasped around her face. She whimpered in protest for only second before wrapping her hands around his neck to hold him tight.

After several intense moments, he broke the kiss, resting his forehead against hers, eyes meeting hers, desire flaming between them both. "I like you, Hope. I find I'm liking you a lot. And even though it's only been two days, this feels really right. And different."

She captured the corner of her lower lip between her teeth to try to stifle the wide smile threatening to break across her face. "I really like you, too." She brought her mouth forward and brushed a chaste kiss across his welcoming lips. "And I like you for everything you are, everything you've shown me about yourself while you've been here. I don't care how much money you make, Gage. Please, don't care about how much I may have either. This, who you see right here, this is who I am."

"I believe you. I do." His mouth turned down in a slight frown. "I learned the hard way that, sometimes, life has other plans for who we are or what we want, though."

She nodded her head slowly. "I know. But let's not let that ruin what we have right now, okay? Before it even happens."

"I have always wanted to fly on a private jet." He grinned slyly.

A slow grin spread across her face. "Good. It's settled then. We'll stay 'til Tuesday."

Chapter Eleven

With breakfast finished and both of them dressed, Hope packed up a small cooler full of snacks and drinks while Gage gathered his camera equipment. They met in the entryway, supplies in hand.

"Hey, what do you think about taking old blue out today?" Hope asked. "It's a stick shift, though, which I'm not very good at, so would you mind driving?"

His face lit up with a wide smile. "That would be fantastic. I can handle a stick, no problem, and I can probably get some great classic shots with the truck."

"That was easy!" She laughed and pointed to a set of hooks behind him. "The keys on are on the blue keychain hanging on that third hook."

He turned and grabbed the set off the hook before reaching down to grab his camera bag and the cooler from her. "Let's hit the road then."

He placed the cooler in the bed of the truck and unlocked and opened the passenger door for her. She turned and gave him a shy smile as he reached to help her up into the truck. "I'm still not used to you opening my door for me like this. It's nice."

"Guess you'll have to keep me around then." He leaned down and pecked her on the lips before closing her door and making his way over to the driver's side and hopping in. He put his camera bag down between them and put the key in the ignition to start the truck. One turn and she came to life with a loud purr. He pressed on the gas lightly to rev the engine.

"You weren't kidding! Walter does do a great job keeping this old girl in shape!"

Hope was smiling widely with pride. "I told you." She pointed back toward the driveway. "If you follow the driveway to the end, then take a right, we'll follow Route 2 down into Charlotte. I'll show you a little covered bridge that's kind of on the side of the lake down there. It's pretty in the fall."

"Okay, sounds good." He headed out in the direction she had directed him, noticing that Walter had cut up the fallen tree that blocked their path the other night. "Looks like Walter's been busy."

"He's so wonderful to have around. He makes sure this place is always in tip-top shape. We're lucky to have him." She reached over and turned the radio on. "Do you care what we listen to?"

He shook his head. "As long as it's not rap, I'm good."

"Oh my God! Me too! I can't stand rap. I call it rap crap.

My brother gets so mad at me because it's all he ever wants to listen to." She scanned through the stations until she found one that was playing a James Taylor song.

"This is perfect," he stated and smiled over at her. They chatted easily about everything and nothing during the twenty-five-minute ride to the first covered bridge. As he rounded the corner of the narrow town road they were on, the bridge came in to view.

"Well, look at that! She's an old beauty!" He pulled the truck into a small turn-off on the side of the road just before the bridge and shut the engine off.

"I told you it was pretty." She opened her door and jumped out of the truck, meeting Gage as he rounded the front of the vehicle.

"Hey, I would have helped you out of the truck." He set his camera bag down on the hood and turned to her.

"You don't have to help me every time we stop. I'm a big girl. I can get in and out of the truck by myself." She smiled over at him.

He stepped closer to her and, leaning down, cupped her cheek lightly as he brushed a kiss across her lips. "But then I don't get to do this." He kissed her again, this time more deeply, both of them stepping into one another's arms. A car, beeping its horn as it drove by, had them pulling apart quickly, laughter tumbling from both of them. "Oops. I guess we don't need to give the townsfolk a show, eh?"

Hope's cheeks were flushed pink, but she was smiling and happy, regardless of being caught in such a passionate moment. "If they want a show, we could give them a flash of those abs of yours." She grinned mischievously and winked at him.

He shook his head laughing and began opening the camera bag and taking his gear out. He quickly changed the lens, made some adjustments to the settings and started walking over to the bridge. She followed along beside him, watching him take in the bridge, the lake, and the overall scene with a calculating eye. He stopped abruptly, brought the camera up to his eye, and started snapping pictures.

She wandered closer to the lake, leaving him to do his thing. There was a small family of ducks just off to the left of the bridge, so she walked closer to see if she could get a better look. Then she made her way onto the bridge itself and found herself looking at all the old initials that had been carved by past visitors. People had been carving their initials in this bridge for as long as she had been coming here. Some people even carved in little poems or sayings.

"Hey," he called from the end of the bridge. She turned to find him pointing the camera at her. "Stay just like that." She obeyed his command and froze, just looking straight ahead at the camera. At some point through his clicking and walking closer to her, she let herself lean up against the side of the bridge, her body relaxing into it.

He finally pulled the camera away from his face and smiled serenely at her. "You are such a breath of fresh air. Do you have any idea how you make the simplest things look beautiful?"

She tilted her head and bit her bottom lip like she always did when she was slightly embarrassed. "Really? I was just reading the carvings."

He had reached her now and ran a hand gently over her hair before resting it on her shoulder. "You're so expressive, though. I could almost see what you were thinking as you read certain things—when one made you sad, or when you thought something was sweet. I love that about you."

Wait? Did he just say he loved something about her? He watched as she clamped onto her lower lip hard enough to draw blood and knew she noticed it, too. *Screw it. It is what it is.*

He reached over and used his thumb to pluck her lip out from between her teeth and kissed her tenderly. "Show me what you were looking at."

"Okay," she answered softly and turned back toward the inside of the bridge. "Look at this one right here. April loves John '56. This has been here for seventy years. Isn't that crazy? I wonder if they're still together?"

She watched as he moved his camera back to his face and took some shots of the carvings before looking back at her again. "Did you ever carve your name here? Or your and some lucky boy's name?"

She shook her head, laughing lightly. "Nope. Do you believe it? I think my mom told me that her and Dad's are carved somewhere on this bridge, though."

"Let's put ours then." He said it before he even realized what he was saying and couldn't help the surprised expression that followed. "I mean, only if you want to."

She cocked her head, just analyzing him for a moment. "Really? You want to carve our names?"

He nodded his head, absorbing the fact that he really did

want to leave his mark with her on this bridge. "Yes. Why the hell not? This has been a weekend to remember."

Her eyes lit up as a delighted smile broke across her face. "Okay! Let's do it!" She scrunched her mouth up and looked at him. "We need something to carve with, though. Any ideas?"

He dug into his pocket and pulled out a small Swiss army knife, holding it up, beaming proudly. "Yep. I think I've got just what we need."

"Oh my God." She shook her head in humorous disbelief. "You seriously have a knife on you."

He shrugged. "I'm a Marine. Always prepared." He started walking slowly down the inside of the bridge looking for an empty space to leave their mark. When he found a place he liked, he stopped and looked over at her, raising an eyebrow in silent question.

"Yeah." She nodded and smiled. "This is the spot."

He handed her his camera and turned back, pulled open the knife, and began carving. His body was in the way, so she couldn't get a good look at exactly what he was carving, but she could see little chips falling to the bridge floor. She tried to be creative and sneak some shots of him carving, but she wasn't certain if she actually got anything good of him.

Every now and then, a car would drive slowly through the bridge, and Gage would stop and pretend to be reading instead. It was silly, actually, because obviously, everyone did this, but it still seemed like they had to do it on the sly.

Finally, he stepped away, and with a wave of his hand and a broad grin on his face, he let her see. "Ta-da!"

Her eyes found his carving, and immediately, her hand came up to cover her mouth as she gave a little gasp of surprised pleasure. Inside a small hollow heart, he had carved Gage + Hope. It was perfect.

She turned back to him slowly and raised her eyes to find him staring at her curiously. "Gage, it's so…" She threw her hands up in the air, and for a moment, Gage wondered if what he'd carved was too much. But then she shook her head, saying, "It's the most romantic thing anyone has ever done for me!" There! She'd said it!

He chuckled at her reaction to such a small gesture but couldn't deny the pleasure it gave him to know how happy he had made her. *When was the last time he wanted to make someone happy?* He honestly couldn't remember. But he knew he wouldn't forget this moment—the moment that made her eyes sparkle like diamonds and her face light up like the sun. Seeing her like this filled him with a sudden, unexpected warmth, causing him to pause for a second. *Was he starting to fall in love with this woman?* His heart rate ratcheted up to break-neck speed as he swung his gaze back over to her again.

She was attempting to take some pictures of the carving with his camera, when she looked up and saw that his face was flushed and he seemed to be breathing heavily. "Are you okay?" Her face filled with concern as she moved to come up next to him.

He nodded gruffly and gave her a weak smile. "Yeah, yeah. I'm okay. I got warm suddenly. Could use some water, I think."

She reached out and placed her palm on his forehead to

check his temperature. He took her hand in his and moved it away but didn't let go. "I'm okay. Really."

"Okay," she replied worriedly. "Let's go get you a water out of the cooler."

He continued to hold her hand, using it as an anchor to keep him from floating away as realization about his feelings for her sunk in. *Could someone fall in love in only two days?* He glanced over at her, and instead of feeling any trepidation, he felt tranquility. *Fuck. He was definitely in love with her.*

They had reached the truck, and Hope was trying to climb up onto the side so she could grab a water out of the cooler for him. Strong hands gripped around her waist, pulling her back off the truck, and she let out a yelp. She was spun around, and Gage's lips were on hers before she could even scold him.

His strong arms enveloped her small body until she was flush with him, her arms slipping up and around to clutch onto the back of his neck. One large hand fisted her hair at the nape of her neck as he deepened their kiss, pushing her back until she bumped into the truck.

He ground his body into hers, his hardened length rubbing into her hip bone. One hand left her body and clutched onto the bed of the truck as he continued to press into her, their lips never leaving each other, their bodies so close they were almost one.

She finally tore her lips from his, panting, and looked up at him. "Where did that come from?"

He shook his head and grinned wickedly. "I told you I was feeling warm." He leaned in and dropped several kisses along her neck, soft hums of approval coming from her. "This is what you do to me."

She pulled back, smiling. "Not that I'm complaining about this sudden ravishing, but we are on the side of the road, and anyone could come by at any moment."

He raised one brow suggestively while grinning. "Not into the thrill of being caught?"

"I think we've had more than enough of that between Walter and my father's phone call yesterday." She cocked her head at him, this time raising her eyebrows.

"Touché." He kissed her on the nose and finally released the hold he had on her by stepping back. "I can't seem to get enough of you. Sorry for the sneak attack."

She looked at him coyly and closed the distance between them by pulling him close to her again. "Don't ever apologize for wanting more of me. That's the best thing I've been told in a very long time." She kissed him then, soft and torturously slow, causing him to groan.

This time, he pulled away. "Woman, unless you want me to throw you in the bed of that truck and have my way with you, you better walk away right now."

She laughed heartily but stepped away and held her hands up in surrender. "Okay, but we're definitely picking up where we left off as soon as we are somewhere private!"

"Deal."

Chapter Twelve

They spent the rest of the morning and most of the afternoon travelling to several more covered bridges in the area, Gage taking pictures at every location. The afternoon was gorgeous, with the sun still shining brightly at three in the afternoon, keeping the temperature comfortable for late September.

"Are you covered-bridged-out yet?" Hope asked as they pulled out and away from their latest visit.

"I think I am, actually." He smiled gratefully at her. "What do you have in mind for us next?"

"Oh, you think you have me all figured out already, huh?" She chuckled.

"Well, you do seem to be a bit of a planner."

"Okay, you got me there." She shrugged sheepishly. "I can't help it, though. It's ingrained from my job!"

"No complaints from me, Little Miss Type A." He gave her a playful wink. "Someone needs to keep us in line."

"Well, there's this place called Top of The World that we could hike up to if you want." She looked at him and then continued. "It's not a real hike or anything. It's a snowmobile trail that leads up to the top of this amazing hill that lets you see the whole valley and the lake."

He looked over at her, grinning. "Let's do it. It sounds gorgeous."

She gave him the directions, and within thirty minutes, they were back in her neck of the woods and she was guiding him through some back roads to the trail head location. He pulled onto the side of the road and parked the truck, hopped out of the truck, and was opening her door before she had time to grab for her handle.

She smiled warmly at him and took his proffered hand, stepping out of the truck and directly into his arms, placing a kiss on his lips. "Thank you."

He smiled back and reached around her to grab his camera bag off the seat. "Okay, lead the way!"

She led them down the road only a short bit before indicating the start of the trail and walked into the woods onto the path. They were quiet most of the hike up the long, winding hill. Every once in a while, Hope would point out a pretty bird or a part of the trail that was rocky or rough. As they neared the top, the light became brighter as the tree line leveled off and allowed more sunshine through.

Hope reached over and grabbed Gage's hand in hers as they crested the top of the hill, excited to see his reaction to the view. She looked over and smiled widely as his jaw dropped open and his gaze swept the horizon.

"Jesus! It's beautiful up here!" His gaze stopped on her, a

smile blooming wide on his face. "This is a hidden gem if ever I saw one."

"I knew you'd like it." She grinned back. "It's one of my absolute favorite places to go. Don't you feel like you are on top of the world?"

He looked out over the horizon again, and Hope watched his face as he took in the sweeping hills leading to a valley nestled below and the little houses dotting the landscape surrounding the lake. The sun was sitting lower in the sky now, and its rays were sparkling brightly on the water. There wasn't a single cloud in the sky, and without the shadows, every color seemed more alive and crisp.

"I feel closer to God here. Is that strange?" He turned toward her.

She shook her head, "No. That's exactly how I feel when I'm here, too."

He turned back toward the view and unconsciously unzipped his bag and had his camera in his hands and up to his face within seconds. She watched as he snapped shot after shot, mesmerized by his singular focus. He was fascinating to watch. She loved how every single thing he did seemed natural and instinctual—without thought. Nothing was preconceived with him, making him and everything he did truly real and believable.

She loved watching how his hands worked, his long fingers focusing the lens causing the muscles on his forearms to tighten. She sighed dreamily as she recalled how wonderful those same fingers always felt on her, and how those same arms had held her and made her feel so wanted and safe over the last few days. She was surprised how quickly they had become so comfortable with each other.

He looked over at her then, snapping several photos of her staring at him before she could react, throwing her hands up over her face. "Oh my God! Stop! You caught me red-handed ogling you!"

"That was definitely a look I wanted to catch and see over and over." He had lowered his camera and was smiling wickedly at her. "It's nice to know you like what you see."

Making her way over to him, she slid her hands around his waist, tilting her head to look up at him. "I like what I see very much."

"Me too." He bent and pressed his lips to hers, one arm draping loosely over her shoulder as he brought the other one up and snapped several selfies of them before pulling away. "Turn around so I can snap us with the lake in the background."

She did as he requested, moving to stand beside him, the gorgeous lake and hills as their backdrop. He held the camera backwards in front of them and clicked off a few pictures. Turning it back around, they looked at the pictures of them, smiling in approval at his efforts.

"Those are so good!" Hope beamed. "You are definitely going to have to send me copies of all of these."

He put the camera back in the bag and placed it on the ground, reaching over to grab her hand and pulling her down to sit with him. "No problem."

She leaned into him as he placed an arm around her, gathering her closer as he bent and placed a kiss on her head, tucking her under his chin. They sat in silence, both content in each other's arms, enjoying the vista that stretched out before them.

~

He let out a long, satisfied sigh and kissed her cheek. "I love—" His heart caught in his throat as he realized what he was about to say, her eyes swiveling up to meet his. "Being here with you."

She stared at up at him, her expression telling him she was trying to read what was happening behind those green eyes of his, and then responded slowly. "I love being here with you, too."

His hand came up and caressed her face, his eyes locked on hers as he lowered his mouth and kissed her slowly. Her hands slid up and around his neck as she reciprocated his actions, her tongue slinking out to graze his teasingly. He hummed his compliance and shifted their bodies so she was beneath him as he lowered her back onto the grassy meadow, her hair fanning her head like a golden halo.

Around them, birds chirped, bees swarmed lazily by, and leaves rustled in the late afternoon breeze, creating a sound-track no man-made music could match. Their kisses continued, the intensity and heat of their bodies building with every stolen breath. Gage dragged his hand down the length of her torso until he found the hem of her shirt and slipped his hand underneath, his palm resting on the silk of her skin. His mouth left hers and started blazing a trail to her neck by nipping his way along her chin, to her ear, and then finally lower, his tongue laving her throat languidly.

She moaned softly as she titled her head back, giving him more access to her throat. His fingertips were brushing circles in a slow rhythmic dance up her stomach, over the mound of her breast, his large hand covering it completely and gently clenching. Her back arched off the ground as she pushed harder into his grasp, her hands gripping his taut biceps.

He lifted his head from her throat to look at her. He nuzzled his nose down over her face before placing a chaste kiss against her lips. "Open your eyes, Hope."

Her lids fluttered open, the pupils dilated and surrounded by a sea of churning blue. She leaned up and bit his lips in a teasing kiss. "Don't stop."

He nipped her back seductively, his tongue snaking out to barely graze over her lips afterwards. "Private enough?" He growled into her ear as he moved his thumb to swipe over her hardened nipple, eliciting a small moan from her.

She turned her head so that she could pummel her lips to his in a frenzied kiss of passion, her hands sliding under his shirt and over his bare back, her nails digging into his skin as he pushed his hardened length against the warm juncture that his body lay against. A hot gasp of pleasure burst from her mouth and into him as her lips broke from his.

"Yes, private enough." She moved her hands around to the front of his jeans, releasing the button, and began trying to push them lower.

He chuckled at her eager efforts and moved his hands down to help her as she moved to do the same to her own bottoms. "Eager, are we?"

Her eyes locked onto his. "I want you." She reached down between his legs and grasped his hard length in her hand, slowly sliding it up and down. "I think this indicates you do, as well."

He groaned and gritted his teeth as pleasure roared through him when her small hand clenched onto his cock. "I've wanted you every second from the moment I wrapped my arms around your perfect body and carried you back to the truck in the rain."

He silenced any further discussion by crashing his mouth over hers, lunging his hips forward, his cock sinking deep, their bodies melting into one.

A little more than an hour later, Gage parked the truck next to the Range Rover back at the lake house. Hope's head was tilted back and resting against the back of the seat, a relaxed smile on her lips as she turned toward him.

"Home sweet home."

He leaned toward her, gripping her lightly at the nape of her neck, and kissed her slowly. Her hand came up and stroked the stubble that had gotten softer with the last few days of growth, enjoying the tranquility a simple kiss from him made her feel. He broke the kiss but moved his forehead to rest against hers, neither of them ready to completely break contact yet. His gaze locked onto hers and seemed to penetrate all the way to her soul, a shiver sweeping down her body.

"What is it?" she whispered in confusion.

"The question is, what are you doing to me?" He blinked slowly, keeping his forehead pressed to hers as he brushed his lips lightly across hers.

Her heart began to race, as if a thousand butterflies were fluttering against her breast, trying to fly away. "I think maybe the same thing you are doing to me."

He kissed her again, this time swiping his tongue across her bottom lip after nipping and pulling it teasingly.

"You are stealing my heart."

Kiss.

"One."

Kiss.

"Surprising."

Kiss.

"Moment."

Kiss.

"At."

Kiss.

"A."

Kiss.

"Time."

Kiss.

Their eyes remained glued to each other, foreheads still together, their breaths mingling together with each heavy exhale. She slid her hand over his heart, feeling the thunder of its pulse under her palm, and rested it there.

"I promise to take good care of it." Her cheeks flushed as her tongue darted out to wet her lips. "As long as you promise to take care of the one you've stolen, too."

His heart stuttered in his chest as her admission sunk home, and just as quickly, a feeling of serenity jumpstarted it back to life. In one quick motion, he wrapped his arms around her and hauled her against him as his lips collided with hers, effectively sealing his promise with a kiss.

When he finally released her, both of them panting, both of them smiling shyly, he shook his head. "I don't understand how I could feel this way after only a few days with you."

She shook her head in return, although it was in agreement. "I know." She peeked up at him through her lashes. "Is it crazy if I keep thinking that I was meant to find you there in the road that night? That even though it seemed like I was rescuing you, it's ended up being you rescuing me?"

He reached up and cupped her face, his thumb stroking her cheek lightly as he answered quietly. "I think maybe we rescued each other."

She faintly nodded her head in acceptance. "Yes, I think maybe we did."

Their lips came together again, tender and full of the feelings they had both just acknowledged, their arms tangled around the other. Gage finally broke his lips from hers and, after one last squeeze, extricated his limbs from hers and grinned down at her.

"Should we go in before we christen ole blue in your driveway?"

Laughing, she slid off Gage and back to the passenger side of the truck. "Probably a good idea. Besides, I'm starving!"

"Good, me too! Let's get inside."

Chapter Thirteen

After a dinner of T-Bone steaks cooked on the grill by Gage, accompanied by fresh tomato slices and baked stuffed potatoes whipped up by Hope, they climbed with satisfied stomachs upstairs to her bedroom.

"Shower?" she asked as she collapsed back on the bed.

He lay beside her, his fingers finding hers and weaving them into his. "Too tired."

"Good." She giggled. "Me too, but I didn't want you to think I was a dirty girl if I was too lazy to shower."

He rolled on his side to face her, a sly smile on his lips. "If I didn't think I'd burst from the dinner we just ate, I'd get you even dirtier."

She placed her hand over her belly and groaned. "Please, if you lay one inch of yourself on me, I think I'll explode."

"What if I light a fire instead? Does that television

work?" He waved his free hand toward the flat screen nestled in one of the bookcases across from the bed.

"It does, but I can only play movies on it. We don't have cable hooked up here."

"Are you going to make me watch some sappy romance movie?" He chuckled as he lifted himself off the bed and moved over to the fireplace.

"What? Do you think girls only like to watch romance movies?" she asked, trying to feign annoyance.

His brows arched high, his lips forming a small grimace. "Uh, yeah."

She sat up, moved over to the bookcase, and began thumbing through some of the DVDs on the shelf. *When Harry Met Sally, Bridget Jones's Diary, Love Actually, Pride and Prejudice, A Walk in the Clouds, The Notebook, Pretty Woman. Shit.* Wait! She found one that might work.

"Ha! How about *For Love of The Game?*" She pulled the case out of the bookcase and waved it in the air triumphantly.

He shook his head, striking a match and setting fire to the kindling, his shoulders shaking slightly as he laughed. "That is a total love story!"

"No, no, it's not!" She moved closer to him, bringing the case to his face. "Look, it's all about baseball." She tapped her finger on the front. "See, baseball player standing on the mound. There's not even a girl on the cover."

Rising to stand in front of her, he reached out and gently extracted the movie from her fingers, bending down at the same time to place a tender kiss on her lips, murmuring, "I don't give a shit what we watch. I just want to hold you in my arms while we do it."

Her lips curled into a smile as she stood on tip-toe and wrapped her arms around him, pulling him into a tight hug. "I love y—"

Her hand flew to her mouth as she stepped out of his arms, an electric shock pulsing through her in one big burst, the blue of her eyes wide and panicked as she looked at him. His mouth was parted slightly, his arms out at his sides, the movie still clutched tightly in one hand as his eyes narrowed in confusion.

"What?"

Did he not hear what she almost said? Holy shit! Had she fallen in love with him? She'd been with Dylan over a year before she said those words to him, and even then, it was only in response to him saying the words. Those words had never just slipped out of her mouth before so naturally. *They'd only known each other for two and half days! This was insane. People don't fall in love over a weekend. Do they?*

"I left the oven on!" she blurted out.

His brow crinkled, his eyes narrowing to slits as he scratched his chin. "Um, okay. Do you want me to go shut it off?"

"Nope, no." She spun around and skittered toward the doorway. "I'll do it. Be right back!"

age shook his head as he watched her scurry out of the room and wondered what the fuck just happened. Did he just imagine it, or did she almost say I love you? He chuckled. She just had a complete freak out, kind of like what happened to him earlier.

He dropped the movie on the bed and went over to the fireplace, grabbing a couple logs and placing them over the kindling. He watched as they caught fire and flames tickled their way up and over the wood, the heat intensifying quickly. Much like his and Hope's feelings for one another. He threw another log on, daring the fire to burn even hotter, wanting to prove he could most definitely handle the heat.

"All set!" He turned his head away from the fire and toward the light voice carrying across the room. "It wasn't on. Guess I'm going crazy."

He placed the screen over the flames and walked across the room to meet her halfway, cupping her face in his big hands and tilting it up to his. "It's okay if you're going a little crazy. I think I might be, too."

He said the words softly, just above a whisper. He hoped that she would understand their double meaning and take some comfort in the fact that he was just as surprised and confused by all of this as she was. His eyes trailed down to where her teeth had captured her lower lip and was chewing it lightly. Her nervous tell.

Cocking one side of his mouth up in a knowing smile, he leaned down and pulled her lip free with his teeth and kissed her deeply. He slid his hands down, one sliding behind to clutch onto the back of her neck, and the other continuing down to the base of her back, where it laid flat as he pushed her up against him. She moaned softly into him as she slid one hand to press against his heart and the other grasped onto his bicep.

He lost himself in the kiss, savoring her taste as his tongue swept against hers, inhaling each breath she panted out through her nose. When he felt her body finally relax and give in to what she was feeling, instead of pushing in fear against it, he closed his mouth around hers one more time and gently pulled away.

She looked up at him, eyes blazing with desire, little pants coming from her kiss-swollen lips as her chest rose and fell in quick bursts. He nipped her lips one more time and smiled broadly at her.

"So, you're completely sure it's just about baseball?"

She rolled her eyes, a smile breaking out across her face as she looked up at him. "Well, mostly."

He kissed the tip of her nose, the smile never leaving his face, then turned and picked the movie up off the bed. "Let's put it in then. I love baseball."

Gage blinked awake as Hope turned and nuzzled herself deeper into his chest. He moved to pull the blanket up over her shoulder and furrowed his brow as he noticed green waves bouncing off her golden hair. He looked up to see if they had fallen asleep with the television on and gasped when his gaze landed on the scene unfolding outside the full-length windows. "Holy fuck!"

Hope sat straight up, bleary eyes trying to open as she shook herself awake. "What is it? What's wrong?"

He pointed to the window, his eyes still locked on what he saw, his mouth open in awe. "Look."

Her dainty hand was rubbing at her eyes as she turned in the direction he pointed. A smile appeared on her face and grew wider as she turned and looked at the awe on his face.

"It's the Northern Lights. You've never seen them before?"

He shook his head back and forth absently, still unable to look away from the spectacle before him. "The Aurora Borealis?" His voice was laced with wonder.

She slid out of bed and stood up, walking over to the front of the windows. "Yes. It's early for them to be out. We usually don't see them until later in the winter."

"You've seen them before?"

"Yes, lots of times." She turned back to him and was overwhelmed with emotion at witnessing the wonder in his face. "Come. Let's go outside so you can see them."

Not breaking his gaze from the view outside, he moved out of the bed and walked to stand next to Hope. "It's amazing. I've read about them and seen photos, of course, but this is just..."

She smiled up at him. "I know. It's something you have to see in person." She bent and picked his sweats and t-shirt up off the floor. "You may want to put these on."

He finally tore his gaze away from the window to look at what she was holding. A grin broke across his face. "Sorry. But wow!"

They both laughed as he quickly pulled his clothes on and sprinted out of the bedroom. "I need my camera."

She pulled on a pair of flannel pajama bottoms and a sweater over the t-shirt she had on, following in his wake. She found him in the living room, changing a lens. He looked up when she walked into the room.

"Can we go out on the deck? Is that okay?"

"Of course." She walked closer to him and giggled at his excitement. Kid in a candy store came to mind when she thought of him in this moment. "Do you want to go down to the dock? It might be even better because you won't have any shadows or lights from the house, and the colors may be clearer."

He stopped what he was doing and looked at her. "You totally get me."

She shrugged her shoulders. "You're an artist. I get that."

He walked over to her and grabbed her face. "You are going to have a really hard time getting rid of me." Then he kissed her hard and quick before turning walking back to his equipment to grab it. "Let's go."

They went outside and walked down to the docks. She watched as he set his camera on a tripod and took what seemed like a thousand pictures. She didn't mind, though. Everything about this night was beautiful—his words, his passion, the lights. When he seemed to be satisfied with the number of photos he had taken, he came over and sat beside her on the dock.

"All done?" She scooted closer and pressed herself against him. He wrapped an arm around her and pulled her close.

"I'm sorry. You must be freezing." He rubbed his hand up and down her arm to try to warm her. "I get caught up sometimes."

"I'm fine. Really. I can't complain about anything when this is what we have to look at. It's so absolutely beautiful."

He rested his chin on the top of her head as he continued to watch the green, yellow, and blue lights slide across the sky. "I can't believe I finally got to see them. It only took thirty-two years."

"They are rare in the states, that's for sure. Some people never see them."

"This has been a weekend of firsts for me." He kissed the top of her head. "One I'll never forget."

"Me neither." She spoke quietly.

"First time I broke down in Vermont."

"First time I picked up a stranger on the side of the road."

"Ah, but what a good-looking stranger he was, right?"

She turned her head up to him and smiled, tickling him in the ribs as she did. "Eh, he's okay."

"First time I carved my name on a covered bridge."

She turned out of his arm and moved so she was facing him. "First time I had my name carved on a covered bridge."

"First time I saw the Northern Lights."

Her face screwed up a moment while she tried to think of another first. Before she could answer, his lips were on hers in a tender kiss and he was whispering against her. "First time I'm telling you that I love you."

"What?" Her question came out in a surprised whoosh as her eyes flew up to meet his.

He leaned down and placed another tender kiss against her lips before speaking again. "I think I'm in love with you."

"Oh my God." Her hand brushed over her lips softly where his just were as she looked up at him again, wonder in her eyes. "I think I'm in love with you, too."

~

Hope groaned in protest at being shaken gently. "Wake up, sleepy head."

Her cheeks rose lazily as soft lips brushed against hers. "Morning, Sleeping Beauty." Hair was lifted away from her eyes as they fluttered reluctantly open.

"What time is it?" she mumbled grumpily, meeting his sparkling green gaze.

"It's almost eleven. You slept late." The aroma of strong coffee had her inhaling deeply and moving to sit up, hands reaching out for the magic elixir.

He chuckled and placed a steaming cup carefully in her grasp. "It's hot and has too much sugar and cream, just the way you like it."

"You really are my Prince Charming." Smiling gratefully at him, she blew on the hot liquid before taking a slow sip. More groaning. "So good. Thank you."

"Welcome." He turned toward the window, nodding his head. "Pouring out. Weather says it's going to last all day."

Turning her head to look at the rain splashing against the windows, she sighed. "Guess we aren't going sailing today." She looked back at him, a sad smile on her face. "Sorry. I really wanted to take you out."

He shrugged and grinned, eyebrows rising. "I can think of plenty of other things we can do." His hand reached out, gently took the mug from her fingers, and placed it on the bedside table.

"Oh, really." She grinned right back. "Like what?"

Waggling his eyebrows and displaying a feral grin, he pounced on top of her, showing her exactly what he meant as he crushed his lips to hers.

Chapter Fourteen

After spending most of the prior day in bed, they'd woken this morning to clear blue skies. Packing her computer back in its bag, Hope looked longingly out the living room windows. "I wish we didn't have to leave. Wouldn't it be nice if we could just hide out here forever?"

Gage wrapped his strong arms around her, relishing the warmth of her body as he pulled her up against him. She smiled and closed her eyes, and he did the same, savoring these last moments at the house. His warm breath tickled her ear as he murmured against her hair, "Absolutely, but I have a feeling your father will send Walter if you stay here much longer."

Spinning around, she wrapped her arms around his neck and looked up into the crinkled eyes she'd come to adore. "I know. But a girl can dream, right?"

Leaning down, he brushed a kiss across her lips and

rested his forehead against hers. "We live a subway ride away from each other."

Feigning shock, she opened her eyes wide. "The subway? That place is scary!"

Pulling back, he shook his head, a grin on his face. "Oh, my little princess… I'll take the subway. You can have your driver bring you." Looking at her, brows raised, he added, "That is, if you aren't too afraid to slum it in The Village."

Slapping him playfully on the arm, she giggled. "Hush, you big brute! I can handle The Village!"

"Yeah, yeah." He threw a playful wink her way. "We'll see about that." He moved to take the computer bag from her and walked out to pack it in the Range Rover next to his already-stowed bags. Coming back into the house, he found her standing across the living room in front of one of the large windows. He watched silently as she lifted her hand and pressed it against the glass, holding it there for a moment.

When she finally dropped her hand, he moved closer and walked up behind her. "Are you ready?"

Twisting to face him, a small smile on her face, she nodded. "Yep. Time to go, I guess."

"Okay. Everything's packed up, so we're good to go." They both started toward the front entrance and looked back one last time before closing and locking the door behind them.

"You want to drive?" She held the keys out to him.

"Sure. You don't want to?" He took the keys from her, following her to the passenger side and opening the door to help her in.

"I want to put all my info in your phone and vice versa." She looked up at him and smiled shyly. "Gotta make sure I can find you back in the big city."

Leaning in, he took her head gently in his larger ones and kissed her, his mouth claiming hers possessively. When he finally broke the kiss, he locked his eyes with hers. "I'm not losing you now that I found you. Don't worry."

Pulling the corner of her bottom lip into her mouth and chewing it, her eyes turned lusty as she tried to conceal her smile. "Okay."

He angled his mouth toward her again, sucking her lip from her teeth and grazing his lips across hers a final time before stepping back from her with a low growl. "You know that drives me crazy."

"Sorry." She peeked up at him sheepishly from under her hooded gaze.

"Uh-huh…" A sexy smile graced his face as he shut her door and then made his way around to his side. After climbing in and fastening his seat belt, he started up the Range Rover. "Here we go."

~

"Here we go…" Hope looked over at him, smiled, and reached her hand out. "Phone."

"You sure are bossy." He shook his head as he dug into his pocket. He pulled it out and placed it in her hand.

"You're just figuring that out?" She took his phone and

swiped on the screen, frowning when she realized the screen was locked. She reached out and bumped his arm gently with the phone, indicating he should take it back.

"You're done?" He glanced over, brows furrowed.

"It's locked. Can you put in your password?" Her hand was still outstretched to him.

"Oh, sure." He nodded at her. "It's zero-eight-zero-eight."

She slowly pulled her outstretched hand back, her mouth falling slightly open. "Really?"

He looked over and then braked, moving to the side of the road to park when he saw her face. "What?"

"You're going to give me your password? Just like that?" she asked in disbelief as she shook the phone at him.

He scoffed and chuckled. "Why not? I don't have anything to hide. It's just my phone."

She looked down at her lap where the phone was now perched before looking up at him, her voice quiet. "Do you know that I was with my last boyfriend for over two years, and I never knew his code. Ever." She frowned while rolling her eyes. "I guess that should have been a sign that he was a total asshat."

He leaned over and swiped a kiss across her lips, staying close for just a moment as he responded. "His loss is definitely my gain."

"And it's stuff like this that makes me fall just a little more for you." Pink flushed across her cheeks at her admission.

His face lit up as a smile broke across his face, and he turned back to the road and took off driving again.

"So, zero-eight-zero-eight? Any significance?" she asked as she typed in the passcode.

"Birthday."

"Yours?" She looked over to get his response.

"Yep."

"You're a Leo." She realized then that she liked thinking of him as a powerful lion. The sign suited him. "I guess we should at least know each other's birthdays by now."

"When's yours?" he asked.

"April fourth. I'm an Aires."

"You're my half." He grinned at her widely.

"What?" Her head tilted and eyes crinkled as she looked back at him.

"I'm zero-eight-zero-eight. You're zero-four-zero-four." His grin grew larger. "My half."

Her eyes locked with his sparkling ones and lit up in return. "Your half."

He broke their connection by turning his attention back to the road, his smile planted firmly. She finally programmed her name, number, and address into his phone and saved it. When it was done, she pulled her phone out of her purse and called herself from his phone. When his number popped up, she cancelled the call.

"Here you go." She extended his back to him, and he took it from her, his eyes never leaving the road.

"Thanks, Angel."

Her heart skipped a beat at his endearment, and she began to add his contact information to her phone but paused. "Gage Flynn, birthday August Eighth. Address?"

"Two-eight-eight Waverly Place, apartment C." He

looked over at her and waggled his brows. "There's a Star-bucks on the corner if you ever want to stop by for coffee."

"Good to know." She laughed as she entered the information. "There! It's official. We're phone friends now."

"Excellent. I expect very naughty texts at least once a day." He gave her a wicked grin followed by another wink.

"Gage!" she exclaimed in mock surprise. "I am so not that kind of girl."

"Oh, I just bet you are." His wicked grin was still in place.

"What am I going to do with you?" She laughed lightly.

"I can text some ideas later."

The rest of the ride was filled with light chatter and music on the radio. As they entered the airport, Hope directed him to the private hanger where the plane was located. She instructed him to park the truck outside the entrance, indicating someone would arrive later to retrieve and store the vehicle for her until the next time she visited.

"This is pretty surreal." He scratched at his stubble as he looked out at the hanger. "I can't say I've ever flown on a private jet before."

"Please, don't feel weird." She reached over and took the hand scratching at his face, grasping it in hers. "It's the company plane. I'm just lucky enough to be able to use it from time to time."

"Still weird." he grumbled back.

She squeezed his hand lightly before letting go. "Come on. Let's get our stuff and board so we can head home."

"Leave the keys?" he asked.

"Yep." She reached for her purse, and they both moved to open their doors. When they met around the back of the truck, he opened the hatch and grabbed their bags then followed her inside the hanger.

As they approached, Glenn strode over, a wide smile on his face, and greeted them. "Hope! You look wonderful!" His eyes darted briefly to Gage and then back to her. "I take it the weekend treated you well?"

She felt her cheeks heat as realization sunk in at how the situation might appear to someone else. "Hi, Glenn. Yes, the weekend was just perfect."

"I'm glad to hear it." He stretched his hand out to Gage. "Glenn Masters. I'm the captain and will be flying you home this morning."

Gage grasped Glenn's hand, giving it a firm shake. "Gage Flynn. Appreciate the ride."

"My pleasure." Glenn reached for the bags Gage was carrying. "Can I take those for you?"

"Uh, sure." He shrugged the bags off his shoulder and handed them over. "Thanks."

"You two are welcome to board. We can take off as soon as you're settled. All pre-flight checks are complete."

"Thanks, Glenn." Hope reached her hand out and slid it into Gage's, twining her fingers through his as she turned and led them to the plane.

He leaned down and gave her a chaste kiss on the cheek, a low chuckle escaping as he murmured, "Fucking surreal."

They climbed the stairs and boarded the jet. She led him through the entry into the main cabin, where he stopped short, jerking her hand as he did. "Whoa."

She turned and, seeing the awe on his face, stepped closer and wrapped her arms around him. "Too bad the flight is only an hour and a half. I could have introduced you to the mile-high club otherwise."

His gaze snapped down to hers, the lushness of the cabin forgotten, a wicked grin appearing. "Oh, I think that's more than enough time to make that happen." He captured her lips in a searing kiss, his large hands cupping her face to his.

"Oh!" A startled voice came from behind them. "Excuse me, Miss Yorke! I had no idea you'd boarded. I'll come back in just a moment."

Two things happened simultaneously, both unexpected. Gage's entire body stiffened in her arms as he pulled back harshly and held her at arm's length, a horrified look on his face. "What did she call you?"

She wasn't sure who to address first, Sylvia or Gage, but he solved that problem when he shook her lightly, demanding a reply through gritted teeth. "Answer me, Hope."

Confusion swirled in her mind. Why was he so upset? And had she not told him her full name throughout the entirety of the weekend? She couldn't recall. And why would it even matter? She stammered out a bewildered reply. "She called me Miss Yorke. Hope Yorke; that's my name."

She watched as he staggered back a step, his face paling as he inhaled a sharp breath and then, under his breath, uttered, "You've got to be fucking kidding me."

She countered and stepped toward him, reaching out as she did, baffled by his reaction. "Gage, what's wrong?"

Both of his arms flew out in front of him, hands up flat. "Stop, Hope. Just stay there for a minute."

She paused mid-stride and froze in place, a look of shock and hurt appearing on her face as she demanded an answer. "What is it? Tell me!"

He shook his head in disbelief, staring up at the ceiling as he raked his fingers through his hair. "Yorke Publishing. That's where you work? Robert Yorke is your father?" He brought dark eyes down to meet hers. "How did I not put the pieces together? You did say you worked for one of the largest publication houses in the city."

"I don't understand." She tried to take a step closer, but he shook his head no. "What difference does this make? How do you know my father?"

"I don't." He wiped a hand down his face in frustration. "Only by association."

"Gage, you're not making any sense." Her voice was beginning to shake with anxiety.

A look of utter sadness swept down his face and filled his eyes as he looked at her. "I'm so sorry, Hope. I can't do this." Then he turned and walked to the exit of the plane.

"What?" Hope's heart literally stopped in her chest, and a cold wave flushed down her entire body before realization smacked her in the face and had her running after him. He was already at the bottom of the steps and asking Glenn for his bags by the time she was at the exit door.

"Gage!" She called to him and started down the stairs after him. He looked up at her, a grimace on his face, as he motioned for Glenn to go get his bags. She was shaking when she reached him and grabbed onto his hand, her voice pleading as she spoke. "Please, tell me what's happening. I don't understand how my father has anything to do with us. Why are you leaving?"

His grip tightened around her small fingers as he pulled her into an embrace. His shoulders drew up, and his chest expanded as he took a deep breath against her hair and exhaled heavily. His hands moved up to the side of her face, which he held gently as he pulled back from her. His brow was furrowed, his eyes crinkled in pain, as he rested his forehead against hers. "Please, Hope, know this isn't your fault. I'm so sorry." He brushed a kiss against her lips as he released his hold on her and then turned abruptly, grabbing his bags from Glenn as he strode toward the hanger's exit.

Hope stood transfixed, her fingertips resting where his lips had just been, tears rolling down her face. She gasped when he stopped suddenly and spun back toward her.

His hand raked through his hair, and he shook his head as if he was having an internal argument, before he finally looked at her. "Ask your father what really happened to your mother." Then he turned and stomped out of the terminal.

Chapter Fifteen

It had been two days, and Hope hadn't heard a peep from Gage. She had texted multiple times, called, and left two voicemail messages. She had even gone as far as having her driver take her to his address in the village, only to have him bring her back home without getting out of the car.

Her father was out of town on business in Miami until the following day, so asking him any questions, at least in person, wasn't possible until then. Discussing her mother's death, and trying to determine how it was connected to Gage, was definitely something that had to be done in person.

In the meantime, she worked from her apartment instead of going into the office. She'd been wearing the same pajamas she crawled into when she arrived home on Tuesday and couldn't remember the last time she'd brushed her teeth. Her eyes felt permanently swollen from the random bouts of tears she would break into every time she thought of Gage. And there was always an open bottle of red wine sitting on her counter, keeping the glass that never seemed to leave her hand full.

She missed him. Her body physically ached to feel his touch and hear his voice again. She didn't even have a picture of him because he was the one who always had the camera. So, instead, she'd spent hours browsing his photography website and, of course, doing Google searches to find any information she could on him. *And why wasn't he on Facebook? Wasn't everybody and their goddamn mother on Facebook these days?*

She'd watched *For Love of the Game* at least four times and tried to remember the parts Gage laughed at, or poked fun at her for tearing up at, and every single time, she ended up in tears. She was torturing herself, but she was at a loss. She'd been with him only four days, but the emptiness she felt was in a spectrum completely different to what she felt when she broke up with Dylan. Love really did suck.

Her phone rang, causing her to practically jump out of her skin. It was after seven in the evening, so she knew it couldn't be work. *Was he finally reaching out to her?* She jumped up from the couch, red wine sloshing out of her glass as she did, and ran to the counter where her phone sat. Swiping it off the counter to look at the caller ID, her heart sank and then instantly started beating furiously. It was her father.

Using her finger, she selected the green accept button and put the phone to her ear, her voice cracking as she answered. "Daddy?"

"Hope?" Alarm was immediately evident in his tone. "What's wrong, dear?"

"Are you still coming home tomorrow?" She sniffled and then inhaled deeply to try and calm herself.

"Yes, I should be back in the city around seven. What's wrong, darling?" She could hear him shifting papers in the back ground. He was always working.

"I need to talk to you about Mommy."

"What about your mother?" The movement on the other end of the phone quieted.

"About how she died. We've never really talked about it, and I have some questions."

There as a long pause before she heard a deep sigh come from the other end of the phone. "Why now, Hope? It's been years since your mother passed."

"Because now it matters. I've met someone, and when he found out who you are, who my father is, he said he couldn't be with me. He said to ask you about how Mother died and then I would understand."

"Hope, this doesn't make any sense. What would your mother have to do with any boy you've met?" Annoyance was starting to lace the very edges of his voice, a warning to her that she was moving into uncomfortable territory for him.

"I don't know, Daddy. That's why I want to talk to you." She took a sip of her wine and continued. "Can we meet for dinner tomorrow when you're back? You can come here if you'd like."

"No, come to the house. I'll have Meg prepare something

for us. Is seven-thirty all right with you?" Meghan was his live-in housekeeper and catered to his every need.

"Of course. Thank you, Daddy." She blinked away the tears that were pricking at her eyes, yet again, this time in relief that she might actually get some answers.

"You don't have to thank me, my dearest. I'll see you tomorrow." She could hear him walking somewhere now and knew he must be on his way to dinner.

"See you then. Love you, Dad." She was about to end the call when she heard his voice again.

"Hope, what's the boy's name? The one who told you to ask about your mother."

She laughed lightly at his use of the word boy. "Daddy, I'm not a little girl anymore, so you should probably stop referring to the men I date as boys."

"Well, you'll always be a little girl in my eyes, so you're just going to have to deal."

She could hear the smile in his voice, and for the first time in days, a small smile formed on her lips. "His name is Gage. Gage Flynn. He's originally from Pennsylvania."

"Did you say Flynn?" he questioned, a new sense of urgency present.

"Yes, do you know him?" Her brow furrowed as she tried to figure out how in the world they could possibly know each other.

"No." His reply was instant and curt. "I've got to go. I'll see you tomorrow. Love you." And then silence.

She turned to look at the phone and saw indeed that the call had ended. *What in the ever-loving-hell was going on?*

Gage slammed the door behind him, dropping his bags to the floor, and walked directly to the fridge and grabbed a beer. Twisting the top off gruffly, he brought the bottle to his lips and emptied it in four long pulls. He turned, tossed the bottle in the trash, grabbed another out of the fridge, and repeated the same process. This time, though, when the second bottle was empty, he gripped it tightly before hurling it across the room, shattering it into a hundred pieces as it slammed into the wall.

"Fuck!" He reached into the fridge and grabbed a third beer. "Fuck. Fuck. Fuuuuuck!"

This time, he took a single pull and walked out of the kitchen, into his living room, and plopped down on his couch. It was only eleven thirty in the morning, but the last twenty-four hours had been a living hell. After walking away from Hope in the hanger, he made his way to the main airport terminal and tried to get a commercial flight back to the city.

Every flight, from all three airlines, was booked going out that day, so he was listed as standby. When a flight still hadn't opened up by six that evening, he'd opted to take a nine-pm flight to New Jersey instead. Of course, given his track record for the day, the plane had mechanical difficulties and had to divert to Boston and land there.

All of Boston's flights to Jersey and New York for the rest of the night were booked, so he ended up sleeping on the floor in the terminal until this morning, when he finally got on a damn flight. He shook his head and took another long pull from his beer when he heard his phone ding. He reached into his pocket and pulled it out, his heart sinking when he saw the notification for a text, the fifth one that day, from Hope ~Angel~ Yorke.

He was afraid to read anything she had sent, afraid he would push all the reasons he shouldn't call her aside and just do it. Because, Jesus, he fucking missed hearing her voice. He missed feeling her in his arms. He couldn't believe his goddamn luck. Of all the women he could have met and fallen for, it had to be Robert Yorke's daughter. He lifted the bottle and banged it against his forehead in frustration before taking another drink.

Gage woke up a couple hours later to his phone ringing, his empty beer bottle clattering onto the floor as he rose from the couch to answer it. Hope ~Angel~ Yorke appeared on the screen, turning his gut ice cold. Instead of answering, he stood there holding the phone and waited to see if she would leave a message. After what seemed an eternity, his phone dinged and 'you have a voicemail waiting' appeared on the screen.

Unable to stand the distance from her any longer, he swiped right to listen to the message. His heart beat furiously as soon as her voice came over the speaker. "Um, Gage? Hi. It's Hope, the girl you spent the most amazing weekend of my life with. I'm not sure what happened or what's happening or why you won't talk to me. Is it weird that I miss you so much?"

There was a long pause, and he thought the message was over, but it suddenly continued as she let out a long, stuttered sigh and began speaking again, this time with obvious tears in her voice. "I don't know what I'm supposed to do now. Will you please talk to me? Or text me? Please. Did I tell you that I miss you?"

This time, the message was over. He stared at the phone for only a moment before he hit the play button again. As hard as it was to listen to the sadness and confusion pouring from her, he could not stop himself from wanting to hear her voice again. After the fourth playback, he jammed the phone in his pocket, grabbed his keys and helmet off the counter, and stormed out his front door.

Flying down the stairs and out the entrance, he turned right and headed into the side alley where he kept his bike parked. He pulled his helmet on as he threw a leg over the leather seat and jammed the key into the ignition. He pressed the start switch and pulled the clutch into gear, revving out and into traffic.

After an hour of driving around aimlessly, he pulled into the parking lot across from the warehouse his friend had converted into a gym. After securing his bike and paying the attendant, he strode across the street to the entrance and made his way inside. He was greeted by the spunky little redhead that often manned the reception desk. His eyes scanned over the back wall, taking in the now familiar name, Baker-Landon-Rose Memorial Gym, and silently said the same small prayer he always did when he came here, for those who had sacrificed their lives.

"Heya, Handsome." The redhead smiled widely. "What can I help you with today? You want to box?"

He shook his head. "Actually, I was looking for Ben. Is he around?"

She nodded while picking up the phone. "Sure is. He's out back with his brother. Let me see if he's available."

"Thanks." His gaze roamed around the gym, watching various workouts and boxing matches in progress as she spoke on the phone.

She hung up and looked his way. "He said he's coming up. His brother is on his way out, so timing is perfect."

"Great, thanks, Stacy." He gave her a small nod and moved over to the seating area to wait.

Not more than two minutes later, he saw Ben's impressive form, and who he assumed must be his brother, walking his way. Ben's face broke into a wide smile when his eyes fell on Gage, and his pace picked up. When he was close enough, he extended his hand, grabbing his in a firm grip, followed by one of those manly side hugs.

"Hey, man! What brings you to my neck of the woods? Haven't seen you in ages." Ben's face was still graced with a welcoming smile, but a touch of concern had his brows raised.

"Just wanted to talk to you about a couple things. Didn't know if you'd be around and was out on the bike so figured I'd stop by." He turned to Ben's brother and extended his hand in greeting. "Gage Flynn. Served overseas with your brother."

He was met with a firm handshake. "Drew Sapphire. Always a pleasure to meet one of Ben's friends."

"Hey! This might actually be cosmic intervention," Ben interjected and pointed at Gage while looking at Drew.

"Gage is a photographer. Maybe he could help you out Saturday?"

Gage tilted his head and looked at Drew. "What's happening on Saturday?"

"We had a new hotel open in the financial district, down on Broadway, and the celebration gala is this Saturday. Our regular event photographer had a family emergency and just cancelled less than thirty minutes ago. Interested?"

"Just like that? You don't even want to see my portfolio?" Gage raised his brows in surprise.

"You're a friend of Ben's. If he says you've got the chops for the job, I trust him." Drew gave his brother a small punch to the shoulder. "It's a pretty easy gig. We really just need someone to capture the usual moments at one of these events so we can throw some pictures in our next publication."

Gage shrugged. "What time you need me?"

"Event starts at seven. Really only need you for the first couple hours. After that, you can hang out, have some drinks, enjoy the hotel. I can set you up with a suite for the night if you want."

"Sounds easy enough, and I'm free Saturday." His chest ached briefly as a reminder of the absence it felt without Hope.

"Wonderful." He reached into his jacket and pulled a card out of an inside pocket, handing it to Gage. "Here's my office number. Call my assistant, Felicia, and she'll set you up with all the event information, a room, and will make sure you get paid."

He took the card and slid it in his back pocket. "Thanks. I'll give her a call in just a bit."

"Thank you!" Drew clapped him on the back. "You're doing me a huge favor and just saved my assistant from having to try to find someone on such short notice." He turned and addressed his brother then. "All right, I'm out of here. If I'm late picking Grace up from school, Hannah will skin me alive!"

A round of goodbyes were exchanged between the three men, and then Ben met Gage's eyes. "What's up? You look like dog shit."

"Gee, thanks, man." Gage shook his head and ran a hand through his helmet hair, realizing he hadn't showered in two days. "Want to get a drink or something? I've got some shit going on and needed to get the fuck out of my place for a while."

Ben nodded. "Sure. I can take off. Let me close my office up and we can head out. Want to hit Kenn's? We can walk from here."

"Sounds good." Anything but being where he might see or hear from Hope sounded fucking perfect right now.

Chapter Sixteen

*W*hat *do you do when you feel like you've lost something that you only just found?* That was the thought going through her head as she sat at her desk for the first time in a week. She wasn't sure why she even bothered coming in. It was after four in the afternoon, and she hadn't made it through a set of manuscript notes or sent a single email.

If nothing else, it did get her out of the pajamas she'd been wearing for days and into a shower and clean clothing. Not that it made her feel any better. She was meeting her father for dinner this evening and hoped that she might finally have some answers. She'd texted Gage several more times but still hadn't heard anything from him.

Was she mistaken in what they had felt for each other? Was it only one-sided? She didn't believe that. She knew without a doubt that he had fallen just as hard for her as she had for him. She stared at the screen in front of her and read her mother's obituary again.

E lizabeth Ann Yorke, of Manhattan, New York, passed away unexpectedly on Sunday, February 21, 2010, due to injuries sustained in a motor vehicle accident.

Mrs. Yorke was the wife of prominent business man Robert Yorke, owner and CEO of Yorke Publishing House. She was the mother to two beloved children; son, Thomas Robert, and daughter, Hope Elizabeth, both residents of Manhattan.

Mrs. Yorke was born in Burlington, Vermont, on January 25, 1962, the daughter and only child of the late William and Margaret Erickson. She was educated in the Burlington school system and met her husband while attending college at New York State University. Mrs. Yorke supported many charitable organizations throughout the city and will be greatly missed.

Relatives and friends are respectfully invited to attend her calling hours on Thursday, February 25th, from 4 to 8 p.m. at the Paul Webster Funeral Home on West 73rd Street. Funeral and Burial services will be private.

In lieu of flowers, donations in her memory may be made to the Robin Hood Foundation, an organization Mrs. Yorke supported throughout her residence here in Manhattan.

. . .

There wasn't a single unusual thing in it. It was much simpler than she would have expected, given her mother's extensive involvement in charities and foundations throughout the city, but she was certain her father was dealing with more emotional things then. There wasn't much more she could seem to glean from staring at the obituary, so she closed it and her laptop and decided to leave the office early.

Three hours later, she walked through the front entrance of her father's building and, after a welcoming nod from the doorman, made her way to the elevator. She pressed the button for the penthouse floor and grabbed onto the handrail as the elevator began its quick climb to the sixtieth floor. Her father kept a house out on the Island but generally spent most of his time in the city for work.

The elevator slowed to a stop, and the doors slid open to a marbled entryway. She stepped out, turned right, and proceeded to his door. There were two penthouse units housed on the top floor, but, of course, her father's faced the Hudson and all its beautiful views. She used her key to open the front door and stepped inside to another beautifully marbled foyer.

"Hello? Anybody here?" she called out as she walked toward the kitchen. When she was almost there, the door swung open and her father stepped through, a wide smile on his face.

"Hope! Hello, dearest." He reached her and placed a dry kiss on her cheek, enfolding her in a brief hug, before pulling away but keeping her at arm's length as he inspected her. "You look tired. I thought the time away at the lake house would be good for you."

"Hello, Daddy." She shrugged and turned out of his grasp then walked to the sideboard against the far dining room wall. It was lined with top shelf scotch, vodka, gin, and red wine. "I need a drink. Do you want something?"

"I'll take a scotch neat. You didn't answer my question." He walked up behind her, took the bottle of wine she had in her hands, and moved to open it for her. She switched tasks and poured a glass of the Glenmorangie she knew he preferred. She passed him the glass as he handed her the opened bottle. After pouring herself a glass, she took a long sip and turned to him.

"The lake house was perfect, exactly what I needed." She sighed deeply and looked past him to the view beyond. The sun had set thirty minutes ago, and the city lights were twinkling in the darkening sky. "Can we sit?"

"Of course." He started toward the living room area beyond the dining room. "Meghan will have dinner ready for us at eight."

"I'm not very hungry. I really just wanted to talk to you about Gage Flynn." She caught the grimace that turned his mouth down for just a moment before he corrected it and nodded. He took a seat in one of the easy chairs as she lowered herself onto the couch across from him.

He took a sip, his eyes peering at hers over his glass as he did, and shook his head as he began to speak. "I didn't think I'd have to hear or say the name Flynn again."

Her heartbeat accelerated, and her posture stiffened at

his admission. "So, you know Gage?" She was sure her voice had come out as shaky as her nerves.

He shook his head. "No, I've never met him, but I know the family."

"Yes, he said to ask you how mother really died. What was that supposed to mean? How is that connected to him?" She watched as her father drained the remainder of the liquid in his tumbler and set it gently on the side table.

When he looked up at her, his eyes were somber and his brows drawn. "This was something I had hoped to never have to share or burden you with, but I suppose there's no choice in the matter now."

He stopped then and turned as Meghan came through the kitchen door with plates and silverware in hand. "Meg, you can set those up in the kitchen if you like. We may be a little while."

"Of course, Mr. Yorke. No problem." She smiled, turned, and went back the way she came.

"Your mother wasn't alone in the car when she had her accident. She had given one of the interns a ride home from the office that day. As you know, the weather was bad, and the student was going home on her own. She was close to your age, I believe. I think your mother felt protective of her."

. . .

He looked at her with a sad smile before continuing. "Anyway, she was also in the car when it crashed, and she died, as well. Although, it wasn't right away. It was a day or two later. Her family blamed your mother for the accident and tried to sue us but lost." He paused and looked at her, his fingers steepled under his chin. "Her name was Faith Flynn. I have to assume that Gage is related to her."

Her mouth fell open in small O as her mind tried to process the information her father had just told her, her hand clutching the material above her shattered heart as she nodded her head before answering in a whisper, "Gage is her brother. I met him up in Vermont, and we spent the weekend together."

Her father's frown deepened as he shook his head and moved to stand and grab his empty glass. "I need another one."

She followed his movements as he walked to sideboard, poured himself a hefty drink, and then took a long drink. Instead of moving back to his seat, he walked past it to stand in front of the window and look out over the city. A million questions were running through her head, but she started with the most obvious.

"How did I not know about this? I wasn't a child when this happened. There wasn't anything in the papers about another person in the car. Does Tommy know about this?"

He turned around and met her with a pained gaze. "Because the girl was the same age as you... It could have been you. I didn't want you to have to go through the pain of dealing with that, as well as losing your mother."

She stood then and began pacing, more questions tumbling from her. "But how did you hide that from me, and then a lawsuit, as well. How could you possibly have kept this out of the news?"

He raised his brows as if the answer was obvious. "Hope, I own one of the largest publication companies in the world. Keeping it out of the news was easy. And then you went back to school where you were busy and away from any of the lawsuit business being handled."

She stopped pacing and moved to stand in front of him instead. "Why would they blame Mother? Why sue us? I thought it was due to icy road conditions. Is there more that you aren't telling me?"

He set his drink down on the table and gathered her stiff body in his arms tenderly while speaking softly. "It was the weather. It was an accident, but they wanted someone to blame. They lost their little girl. You didn't need to deal with all of that."

She pushed herself out of his embrace and looked up at him. "But now I do have to deal with this. I've fallen in love with this man, Daddy. I had no idea that there was a connection to our family, and he feels like I fooled or betrayed him. He won't talk to me or return my calls."

"What do you mean? You've fallen in love? With this Gage Flynn? How and when could this possibly have happened? You've only left Dylan a couple weeks ago."

She gritted her teeth and felt her skin grow warm at the

thought of having to defend her feelings but even more so about discussing Dylan. "Yes, Daddy, I left Dylan after I caught him sleeping with another woman. You seriously didn't expect me to stay with him after that, did you? I'm sorry if it means you're a man short of your foursome for Sunday golf games."

His voice was raised ever so slightly in anger, but his tone was calm as he replied. "Of course, I didn't expect you to stay with him. My daughter deserves better than that. But am I expected to believe you fell in love with another man in the span of time since you left Dylan?"

"You've told me on more than one occasion that you fell in love with Mother the moment you laid eyes on her. Is it so preposterous that the same thing could happen to me?"

She watched as he turned and swiped his glass off the table, bringing it to his lips for a drink before continuing. "Hope, nothing would bring me greater pleasure than to learn you've truly fallen in love. But don't you think you should take some time to let your heart heal before giving it to someone else so quickly? Besides, what do you really know about a man you've only spent a few days with?"

A small, sad smile fell across her lips. "Daddy, the one thing I learned in the past week is that I had no idea what real love felt like until I met Gage. My heart is fuller after spending four days with him, and now more broken, than it could have ever been with Dylan."

He shook his head and turned back to the window. "I think you're making a mistake, Hope. It's too soon. Maybe things are better this way. Do you really want his dead sister coming between you? You will only serve as a constant reminder to him of what he's lost. Sometimes, there are some obstacles that people can't move past, and it's just better to let go and move on."

Her heart skidded to a stop as she listened to her father telling her to give up and move on. "But I love him."

He turned around and stepped to stand in front of her. "Sometimes, love isn't enough. I'm sorry, Hope, but it sounds like he's already made up his mind."

Tears slid from her eyes as her father's words sunk in and travelled straight to her heart, filling the cracks like cement and turning it to stone.

Chapter Seventeen

Gage eyeballed his reflection in the mirror one final time before grabbing his camera bag off the bed, exiting the suite Drew Sapphire's assistant had reserved for him. He hated wearing a suit, but pair it with a tie, and the dislike factor ratcheted up another twenty degrees.

Swanky affairs were not up his alley. But it was Ben's brother, and he'd always help a brother in need. Marine motto and all that bullshit definitely had its benefits, but he wasn't putting this one at the top of his list. He didn't care how nice the comped suite was or how unbelievably tasty the steak was that he'd had for dinner.

The elevator swished open and he stepped in, nodding at other well-dressed people already in the car. After two more stops, the doors finally opened on the ballroom level, and all but one person stepped out onto the royal blue carpeting leading to the grand ballroom.

The one saving grace was his camera. He could hide behind his lens and stay in the shadows as he captured the shots requested. He figured he would need to stay an hour tops before going back to the room and emptying the mini-fridge of all alcoholic beverages while enjoying some free porn. Anything to try to keep his mind on something besides Hope.

He took his camera out and started walking the perimeter of the room, capturing people in various candid shots on the dance floor, at the bar, in animated conversations, or just mingling. He tried to capture the beauty of the atmosphere made more elegant by the floral arrangements, sculptures, and lighting within the room. As he was taking some photographs of a stunning waterfall built into one of the walls, he felt a clap on his back.

"Hey, man. How's it going?" Gage swung around to find Ben holding two beers, one extended to him. He took it gratefully and took a long swig.

"Thanks." He grinned appreciatively. "It's good. Easy shooting. Think I'm just about done. Just waiting to capture your brother's welcome speech and I'm gonna wrap up."

"Yeah, I think he's going on in just a few." Ben took a drag from his beer. "Thanks again for doing this. I know Drew really appreciates it."

"It's not a problem. It's good easy work." He pulled at his tie and grimaced. "Just wish I didn't have to wear this damn thing. Hate shit on my neck."

Ben chuckled and shook his head. "Toughen up and quit your bitching."

"Shut the fuck up with the bitching talk. Where the hell's your tie?"

"I'm not working for my brother, so I'll wear whatever the hell I want." Ben chuckled again and took another swig from his beer. "Looks like Drew is heading up to do his speech now." He pointed his bottle toward the podium on the stage. "I'll let you get back to it. Look me up after if you want to have a drink."

"Will do." Gage drained his beer and set the bottle on a nearby table. "Thanks for the beer."

He walked over to get into a better position for the speech and froze as his eyes fell on the last person he thought he would see tonight. She was speaking to another woman, also blonde, also beautiful, but only a shadow in the light that shined as Hope. She hadn't seen him, so he stepped into the shadows and raked his eyes over her beauty.

Hope was wearing a black cocktail dress, but it was anything but simple. The top was made of lace that hugged her torso and plunged into a deep V in the front and back, flowing into a chiffon skirt that fell right at the knee. The shoes were what made his knees weak, though. Black four-inch heels with satin ribbons that tied around her ankles—sexy and sweet all tied up in one pretty bow. Her hair was loose and curly, swept down and behind her shoulders, falling down her back. Diamonds graced her neck and fell from her ears. Rich red lipstick lined her mouth in sharp contrast to the light blue of her eyes.

He didn't want to take his eyes off her, but Drew had begun speaking and he needed to get some shots. He moved slowly out of the cover of darkness, closer to the stage, and began taking shots. After capturing several, he swung the camera toward Hope and started clicking continuously. He wanted to capture every look that crossed her face. He zoomed in to capture her eyes and sucked in a breath as he realized she was staring straight at him.

He lowered the camera in slow motion, his eyes locking with her shocked ones, his feet seemingly glued to the floor. Time seemed to stand still around him as every sound in the room was muffled out by the roaring of his hammering pulse. He finally broke out of his shocked trance as the champagne glass she was holding slid from her fingers and crashed to the floor, sending shards of crystal scattering in every direction.

Everything in the next moment seemed to happen at once. Drew finished speaking abruptly and left the stage to join the woman who was standing beside Hope. Ben appeared out of nowhere and was suddenly standing next to Drew, both of them directing the ladies to stand still and avoid the broken glass. Drew's assistant, Felicia, arrived with two waiters armed with a broom, dust pan, and a mop, and they began cleaning up the mess instantly.

Gage's feet finally lodged free of the cement they seemed to be encased in, and he moved to join the crowd gathered around Hope, gently grasping onto her elbow as he reached her. "Are you okay?"

Her eyes turned and burned into his, anger seething from them as she hissed under her breath, wrenching her arm out of his hold. "Oh, now you're concerned about how I am?"

Before he could reply, Ben interjected. "Wait, Gage, you know Hope?"

He nodded and raised his own question in return. "How do you know her?"

"Excuse me!" Hope spat out. "I'm right here. Does anyone want to ask me anything?"

Ben raised both hands apologetically. "Sorry, let me start over." He looked down at her with a sarcastic smile before turning back to Gage. "Hope, how do you know my friend Gage here?"

She glared at him before sliding her fury over to Gage. "None of your business." Then she turned her back to both men and addressed Drew and his wife instead. "Drew, Hannah, please accept my apologies, but I think I'm going to call it an early night."

Gage listened as she exchanged pleasantries with the couple and then followed her when she walked away. He threw his camera bag over his shoulder and quickened his gait to catch up and walk beside her. Her head turned, her brows raised in shock, when she realized he was following her. Instead of stopping, she looked forward, increasing the speed of her stride, and headed out of the ballroom in the direction of the elevators.

"Hope, will you stop, please?" Gage reached for her arm and grasped onto it lightly, trying to pull her to a halt. She jerked it out of his hold and continued to the elevator, smashing her finger on the down button when she finally stopped.

He stepped in front of the elevator into her line of vision and was about to speak again when he noticed she was blinking rapidly, trying to stop the tears that were about to fall from her eyes. His heart seized at the thought of causing her more pain, and without thought, he moved to pull her into his arms instead. At first, she fought against his embrace, but after thirty seconds of him not releasing her, he felt her body relax into him and soft sobs vibrate against his chest.

He pulled her against him tighter and ran a hand down her long tresses, trying to calm her. "I'm so sorry, Hope. So sorry. The last thing I wanted to do was hurt you."

The elevator door slid open, and he moved slowly backward into the elevator, not releasing her from his grasp, and hit the button for the twenty-sixth floor. As the elevator started to climb, Hope pulled her face from his chest and looked up at him. "Where are we going?"

"My room."

"Your room? You're staying here?" She tried to pull away from him, but he held her caged in his arms. "I just want to go down and call my car, please."

"No."

"No?" She struggled a little harder this time to get out of his arms, but she was no match for his strength. "You're not going to let me go?"

"No."

"No?" Her voice raised in pitch and concern.

"No." He looked down at her face then, mascara smudged from her wet tears, her lipstick smeared slightly from rubbing against his suit, and he still thought she was the most beautiful thing he ever saw. "Not yet."

A long sigh left her lips as they fell at the corners. "Please, don't do this to me, Gage."

Before he could reply, the elevator stopped, and the doors swished open to his floor. He turned her so she was huddled into his side and held her as he exited and led them to his room. He pulled his room key from his pocket and swiped it over the sensor, the green light illuminating, indicating the door was unlocked. He turned the handle and then pushed the door open wide and guided her through.

As the door shut behind them, he turned, raised her arms above her head, and pushed her back against the wall. His fingers circled around her wrists, his arms bent at the elbows pressed next to hers, his face hovering inches above hers.

Her chest was heaving as quick breaths fell from her parted lips, her eyes wide as she returned his gaze. "Gage, what are you doing?"

He leaned forward then and ran his nose along the base of her neck, grazing over the diamonds that decorated it as he moved toward her ear, inhaling her scent as he went. Growling softly, he nipped her lobe and whispered, "There are so many things we should probably talk about, but right now, all I want is to taste you."

A low moan escaped from her mouth as he grazed slow kisses across her cheek before landing on her lips, ending any possibility of further discussion. His grip tightened around her delicate wrists as he pushed himself closer to her body, one of her legs sliding between his, the other falling open. His tongue plundered hers, ravishing her mouth, small whimpers escaping each time he pushed his arousal against her core.

He tore his lips from her mouth and peppered tiny kisses over her chin, down her neck, to her clavicle, and further down until he reached the bottom of the V of her dress. As he moved lower, he released the grip he had on her wrists and let his fingers brush languorously down her arms and over her chest until they found her breasts. His tongue darted out and traced the lace trim up the inside of the plunging neckline until he reached the swell of her breast. Using his teeth, he peeled the fabric back, exposing her nipple. He placed his mouth over the raised peak and swirled his tongue around the tip, leaving it damp. Leaning back, he blew softly, causing the nub to grow tauter. Her hands clenched onto his biceps, and a groan rolled from her lips each time he swept his tongue over the tip again.

"Gage, please." Her hands moved to grasp onto his hair, and she jerked his head up to hers, meeting his lips with her own, thrusting her tongue deep into his mouth in desperation. He reached down and grabbed her thighs, hoisting her up against his waist, and turned to walk through the sitting area into the separate bedroom. Her arms snaked around his neck, holding tight, her lips never leaving his.

When he reached the bed, he leaned her back and extracted himself from her grasp. He stared down at her as he tore his jacket off and stretched the tie up and over his neck. Not even bothering to unbutton his shirt, he just gripped the bottom and jerked it over his head in one fluid motion.

She sat up and began to work the buckle on his belt, her

eyes fixed on the bulge straining the material under his slacks. His hands stroked her hair back at the same time she yanked his pants down over his waist, his cock springing free. He clenched her hair and wound it around his fist as he felt the heat of her mouth slide down over his length. A guttural moan rose up from his chest, and his head rolled back on his shoulders, his grip tightening on her hair as she glided her tongue up and down his hard shaft. When he felt her lave her tongue flat against the top of his crown, he thought he might come right then.

"Fucking hell. That feels amazing."

"Hmmmmm." She hummed in response as she sucked him back into her mouth and wrapped her tiny hand around his base, gripping it firmly as she continued working her way up and down his length.

He was so close to coming, but when he did, he wanted to be buried deep inside her, so he pulled on her hair, dragging her mouth off his cock. She looked up at him with dark, lust-filled eyes, questioning, a frown forming on her parted lips.

"I want to be inside you." He wrenched her head back further and captured her mouth with his, worshipping the very lips that just surrounded his cock. He nipped at the swollen bottom lip she loved to chew and released her hair to cradle her face as he ended the kiss more softly.

"Stand up." He took her hand and helped her to rise up off the bed.

She moved to drag her hands down his chiseled abdomen, but he stepped back and shook his head no as her mouth dropped open in surprise.

"Take your dress off."

Her eyes darted up to meet his burning ones and, without question, moved her hand to the side of her dress and brought the zipper down. Next, she pulled her arms out of the lacy sleeves, causing the dress to fall down and pool at her feet. She stood before him in only a pair of black silk panties, her diamonds, and those sexy fucking shoes.

His own pants had fallen to his ankles, so he stepped the rest of the way out and moved to stand in front of her. As he came closer, her neck craned back to keep her eyes locked on his. Her teeth had captured her lip and were keeping it prisoner again. He lifted his hand and, using his thumb, pulled her lip free. He shook his head and grinned wickedly.

"I don't need anything else distracting me right now, especially that mouth."

"Sorry." It came out as a breathy whisper.

"No apologies, not yet." He reached forward and pushed her hard enough for her to fall back onto the bed, a yelp coming from her as she landed.

"Stay." He crawled over her, causing her to fall back on her elbows and then her back as he loomed over her. "Relax."

He lowered his head and pressed a soft kiss to her lips before moving to kiss her nose, her chin, and then the small crevice at the base of her neck. He kissed a trail down her torso, stopping to pay extra attention to each breast, her fingers threading through his hair as he moved lower. His tongue circled the small diamond that sat in her navel and then traced to the seam of her panties before his fingers gripped the edges and slid them down and over her shoes.

His kisses began again on the inside of one thigh, pushing her legs open wide as he climbed higher and higher. When he reached the juncture where they met, he kissed her there, both of them moaning in unison.

"I've missed you so much." He planted one final kiss to her thigh before sweeping his tongue inside her folds, feasting there until her entire body was quivering in ecstasy.

"Oh my God! Gage, please, it feels so good. Don't stop." Murmured cries came from her lips as he ravished her. When he felt her about to detonate, he pulled his mouth away and moved up her body, slamming his wet mouth over hers, and with one move, thrust his cock into her pulsing core.

Her mouth formed an O as her body rocked against his, her eyes watching his every movement, her nails scoring the skin on his back as she gripped onto him. His cock swelled larger as he felt her pussy tighten around him and grip it like a vise. He rose and pushed her knees up until he could wrap his hands around her silk-tied ankles and drove into her even harder. Sweat ran down his forehead and dripped down his chest as he felt his body tighten.

"Yes, yes, yes!!" Hope was yelling and her head rolling back and forth on the bed. "Like that. Harder, Gage! Fuck me harder!"

He tightened his grip on her ankles, and with one more brutal push, he pounded into her, his release roaring from him and into her as they both let out shuddering yells of pleasure.

Chapter Eighteen

ope lowered her legs slowly back to the bed as Gage loosened his grip around her ankles, his cock sliding free as he moved to lay on the bed next to her. She arched her back as he slid an arm under her and pulled her flush to his body, a sigh of approval rumbling from his chest that her head now lay on.

"Did I hurt you?" The hair against her cheek vibrated as he spoke and caused her nose to tickle. She wasn't sure how to answer his question. Did he mean in general or in this moment? She went with the later.

"No." She always felt shy after she had sex, and it was no different with him. She liked that he was rough with her, took control of her, but didn't know how to voice that once the act was over. "It was good."

"Good?" He chuckled. "I can probably do better than good."

"Okay, it was really good. Is that better?" This time, it was her turn to giggle.

"I was going to go with fucking amazing, but really good gives me room for improvement."

She scoffed and pinched his nipple playfully in retort. "Smart ass."

He swatted her hand away from his sensitive peak and rubbed it gingerly. "Ouch. That hurt."

"Oh, stop being a baby. You've done much worse to mine."

"Yes. Yes, I have, but I don't believe I've heard any complaints."

She rolled over so she was lying on her stomach facing him. "I do have a complaint, actually."

His brows drew up in curiosity. "Do tell, because I seem to recall only moans of satisfaction coming from you in the last few minutes."

She knew he thought she was still talking about the sex, which she would absolutely agree was fucking amazing, but she wasn't anymore.

"I'd like to know why you never returned any of my calls or texts."

He closed his eyes and let out a low groan as he raked a hand down over his face. "I was hoping we could put this conversation off and live in this bubble just a little bit longer."

She was silent for a moment, contemplating his request, but knew in her heart she needed more answers from him. She decided to compromise slightly and see if she could learn more about his presence at the party this evening.

"Were you working at the party this evening? You seemed to know Ben and Drew."

He reached out, and she watched as he brushed a strand of hair that had fallen across her eyes out of the way, and then he swiped the pad of his thumb across her lip longingly before he replied. "I know Ben. We were stationed at the same location together. My unit went out with his quite often. He was a couple years older than me and looked out for me. I didn't meet his brother until the other day. Their regular photographer had some kind of emergency, and they asked me to fill in."

Her chin rested in her hands and bounced up and down as she nodded. "So, it was a last-minute thing."

"Yeah, Ben asked as a favor." He shifted to move on his side and asked her a question. "How do you know them? Work too?"

"Yes and no. Our fathers are friends and do business together, so I've known both Ben and Drew most of my life, but we also handle all their hotel publications, so I was actually here professionally this evening."

She couldn't help but notice the shadow that crossed his features when she mentioned her father and their company, and she let out a tired sigh. "I spoke to my father, Gage. I asked about what happened to your sister. I had no idea she was with my mother at the time of the accident. He hid it from me."

He grunted and rolled his eyes as he rose off the bed and walked to the end, finding his boxers on the floor and pulling them on. "Yeah, I'm sure he did. I would, too."

She sat up, following his movements, her head tilting,

her eyes narrowing in confusion. "I don't understand." She felt very naked and also got up and, finding his dress shirt, pulled it right side out and put it on. "I mean, I understand how upsetting it is to lose your sister unexpectedly like that, but why would you have kept it hidden, too?"

Gage sat back down on the end of the bed and shook his head. "What exactly did your father tell you?"

Hope went and sat next to him. "He said my mother was in the office that day and offered to give your sister a ride home because the weather was getting worse. Apparently, she was an intern there. Mother's car slid on the icy roads and crashed on the way. My mother died at the scene, and your sister lived for several days but eventually died."

He nodded his head. "And what else? Why did he keep it from you?"

He was insinuating something more in his questioning, but Hope couldn't figure out what, so she continued. "He said that the girl was the same age as me, and he felt dealing with my mother's death was enough. He didn't want to burden me with the girl's death, as well. Your sister, Faith, that is."

His lips tightened in a grimace as he shook his head in disgust. "That's it? Nothing more?"

"That's it." She grabbed his hand and pulled it into hers. "Except that he made me understand why you pushed me away. How seeing me, and my connection to Faith's death, would only serve to act as a reminder of what happened to her and cause you constant pain. When he made me realize this, I at least finally understood why you pushed me away without explanation. I didn't like it, but at least I felt like I had some kind of reason."

He squeezed her hand gently, his eyes meeting hers, sadness rimming their edges. "Hope, there's more to this story than he's told you." He stopped and let out a long breath, shaking his head regretfully. "And I'm not sure if I should be the one to tell you."

"You have to tell me. If there's more, I want to know." She dropped his hand as she stood up and began pacing at the end of the bed. "Gage, please, how can we move ahead if I don't know everything?"

"Because, I'm afraid what I'm going to tell you is not only going to change the relationship you have with your father, but that it will also change the way you look at me. I'm not sure if I can bear that. I don't want to be the one to reveal this kind of betrayal to you."

She stopped short and whirled to face him. "You speak of betrayals and lies and expect me not to want answers? Gage, just tell me. You must."

"Let's go in the sitting area then. If you keep pacing back and forth in my shirt and those heels, I'm afraid this conversation's going to take an entirely different direction." He stood up then. "Come on. I'll make us each a drink. I think you're going to need it."

"Okay." She spotted her panties on the floor and grabbed them, sliding them on before following him out to the two couches that were in the main area of the suite. He had opened the mini-fridge and was scanning the contents.

"What do you want? We always drank wine at the lake

house." He turned and looked at her. "Do you want me to order a bottle?"

She pointed to the small clear bottles on the door of the fridge. "I'll take Grey Goose on the rocks. Do you have ice?"

"I'll get some." He walked over, grabbed the bucket off the counter, and headed for the door.

"Um, no." Hope stood in front of him and held her hand out. "You are not going out there in just your boxers. Put a shirt on. No one is getting to see that body but me while we're here."

He chuckled but complied and walked back into the bedroom, emerging a minute later wearing gym shorts and a t-shirt. "Better, Mom?"

"Much." She grinned. "Thank you."

Ten minutes later, they were seated on the couch, both of them nursing a vodka on the rocks. He took a deep breath and began, watching as she took a sip of her drink. "I just want to state for the record, one more time, that I'm not sure if this is going to make things better or worse. And I know this is going to sound bad, but knowing you knew nothing about my sister makes it easier for me to be here with you right now."

She lowered the glass from her lips as concern seeped deeply into her eyes. "Gage, you're starting to scare me now. Just get on with it."

"Okay, here goes." He took another quick sip. "Your dad was telling the truth when he said my sister was working at your office. She was in art school in Brooklyn on a scholar-ship and got an internship working in one of your design departments."

Hope nodded her head. "Yes, that's very common. We generally offer five internships a year and send out requests to all the local art schools."

"Faith was really excited to work for Yorke Publishing. She loved graphic design and said the creative department was very liberal and invited her to submit her work at any time. I was deployed at the time, but she wrote me emails almost every day telling me about her time here in New York."

Hope smiled wistfully. "It sounds like you had a really close relationship with her."

"Yeah, I guess we did. It was just the two of us, and Irish families tend to be close, I think. We probably get in each other's business more than we should, which brings me to the next part of the story." He took another sip of his drink and went on. "After writing me nearly every day for months, all of a sudden, I didn't get an email for almost six weeks. When she finally responded to all of my worried notes, it was to tell me that she had fallen in love. Then, she went on to tell me that it was to a married man, but she couldn't stop herself from seeing him because he made her so happy."

Gage watched as Hope's breathing seemed to falter, her cheeks growing pink, her head shaking slowly back and forth as she began to put together the pieces of the puzzle he'd been relaying to her. "No. Please, tell me it's not who I think you're going to say."

He put his drink down on the coffee table and slid down the couch to be closer to her. Speaking softly, he confirmed her guess. "Your father, Hope. She had fallen in love with your father."

Dismay sprang to her eyes as they widened in disbelief. "How? I don't understand? I know he loved my mother. He would never cheat on her!"

"It's the oldest story in the book. Pretty, young new secretary falls for older, sophisticated man. How is that not flattering to both of them?"

She still shook her head in denial. "I don't believe it. He wouldn't do that. He's not that kind of man."

He took her face gently in his hands and looked into her eyes. "Hope, she sent me pictures of them. He took her with him to a conference in Miami. They went sailing, had dinner on the beach. I'm sorry, but it's true."

"I don't understand. I know he loved my mother completely." She looked at him, her eyes filled with grief, cracking his heart open just a little more for her.

"I don't think he felt the same about Faith that she felt for him. She was young, naïve, and so inexperienced. I'm sure she believed she was in love, and maybe he told her he was, too. I don't really know because there was a lot that she didn't tell me."

"I still don't understand how she came to be in the car with my mother then. Did my mother know about the affair?"

"I think so, but I can only make assumptions based on the little information she told me leading up to her death, and the lies that your father has tried to tell me.

"Wait, you've met my father?" Shock bloomed over her features.

"Yes, when I came home for Faith's funeral, I confronted him. I wanted answers about what really happened."

"So, tell me, what happened?"

"About two weeks before Faith's death, she sent me an email and told me that she was no longer seeing Robert." He looked at her and clarified to be sure she understood. "Your father." She nodded that she understood, and he continued. "She said he had told her the affair had to end as it was getting too involved and he didn't want to hurt your mother."

Hope scoffed and muttered under her breath, "A bit late to be worrying about that, wasn't it?"

"Yes, I think so. Anyway, a week or so later, Faith actually called me, which she never did. It wasn't easy getting calls overseas. I never knew where I was going to be day to day, but she managed to get lucky and catch me on base. When I finally got on the phone and said hello, she started crying. I was terrified that something had happened to one of our parents, but when she could finally speak, it was to tell me that she was pregnant."

Hope's hand flew to her mouth as she gasped in surprised horror. "What? Pregnant?" Her eyes flew open wider as the next thought crossed her mind and flew out of her mouth. "And it was my fathers? Are you sure?"

He spoke quietly. "Faith had only ever been with one other person, her high school boyfriend, and that had been three years prior. I'm quite certain it was your father's. Although, he didn't believe that and told her as much when she told him. Called her a gold digger and accused her of trying to trap him. She said she pleaded with him and even showed him the date of conception to prove it was his. She was already almost five months along at that point and knew it was a girl."

"Your poor sister. She was so young. I can't imagine what she must have been going through." She looked up to meet his eyes and could see how hard this was to talk about with her, and then a thought struck her. "Oh my God, Gage. Do you know what that means? Your sister was pregnant with my half-sister. What does that make you to me?"

"It doesn't make me anything because the baby was never born and Faith is dead." His words weren't meant to sting, but they did.

"I'm sorry, Gage." She spoke the words as if it was her fault his sister had died.

"You have nothing to apologize for, Hope. But perhaps your father does. Maybe if he had treated her differently, maybe she and your mother would still be here today."

"So, my mother did learn about the affair?"

"This is the part I don't have all the facts to. Faith sent me an email the day before the accident and told me that Robert was insisting she get an abortion, saying he would take matters into his own hands if she didn't. She said she would never abort the baby that far along and was going to contact his wife and tell her about the baby. Faith thought, if your mother knew, she would leave your father and then he would go back to her." Gage shook his head. "Like I said, she was very young and naïve."

"I don't know what happened after that. The next news I heard was from my captain, informing me my sister had been in a car accident and wasn't expected to live. By the time I arrived back in the states, she was gone."

"But you asked my father. What did he say?"

"He actually told me the same story he told you, that his wife had given her a ride home due to the bad weather. What he didn't know was that I knew about the affair and the baby. And when I told him I knew, he denied it all. How can a man turn his back on a woman carrying his child? He knew he had a daughter coming into this world and wanted my sister to kill it so it wouldn't interfere with the picture-perfect life he had already created for himself."

Hope began to shiver as the words he spoke about her father sunk in, and slow, fat tears slid down her cheeks as she finally, once and for all, understood why Gage left her at the airport that day. Not only did her father destroy a young girl's belief in love and happily ever after, he had also just destroyed hers.

Chapter Nineteen

ope brushed the tears off her cheeks and rose from the couch. "I should go."

Gage stood abruptly and took hold of her hand. "What? No! Stay. I don't want you to leave."

Shaking her head, she smiled wistfully and, pulling her hand from his, began walking toward the bedroom. "It's better this way."

He trailed behind, hot on her heels. "What's better this way?"

She entered the bedroom and picked her dress up off the floor, shaking it to try to smooth out some of the wrinkles. She hated that she had to put it back on, but she certainly couldn't leave wearing his shirt. She looked up at him and excused herself as she walked past him into the bathroom, shutting the door behind her.

She set her dress on the counter and began unbuttoning

his shirt, unable to stop herself from burying her nose in the collar to inhale his scent just one more time. She wanted to sear it to memory, no matter how painful the burn may feel later. As she unfastened the last button, she slid the shirt off her shoulders and hung it on a hook fastened to the wall. She stepped into her dress, adjusting it into place, and pulled the zipper up slowly.

She should leave now. She was dressed. Why couldn't she get her feet to move then? She looked at her reflection in the mirror and gazed at the hollow shell staring back. Five short days ago, her heart felt as if it would overflow with the love she had let herself believe in, and now, she felt gutted. She was being punished for the sins of her father—a father she had always loved and admired.

A soft knock sounded at the door. "Hope, you okay in there?"

She snapped her eyes away and opened the door briskly. "I'm fine. Just getting dressed."

He moved to let her exit the bathroom but then stepped back in front of her, causing her to almost fall into him. "Please, don't go. Let's talk and figure this out." He clutched her shoulders gently to steady her and looked surprised when he was met with a cold stare.

"It's better if I leave now and just face the inevitable. Staying with you tonight will just make it harder."

"Make what harder?" he spat out, frustration boiling its way to the surface.

She rolled her eyes and blew out a long breath. "Gage, we can't be together. Not tonight. Not tomorrow. Not ever. I didn't understand what happened on the jet, and still didn't understand why we couldn't overcome the obstacle of the accident after hearing my father's story. But now, hearing your story, after what my father did, I understand. I understand all of it."

He shook his head and raked his fingers through his hair. "Hope, I don't want to lose you. Seeing you tonight, being with you tonight, made me realize how much I need and want you. I don't want what your father did to ruin what we could be. Why should we let him ruin yet another romance?"

"And how would you introduce me to your parents? Or to your grandparents? Do you really think that, every time you say or hear my last name, you won't think of my father and get angry and not be able to take some of that out on me?"

He stared at her, dazed and silent.

"See? You can't even deny what I'm saying because you know it's true. And, Gage, he's my father. No matter what he did—and believe me, I think it's horrible and disturbing on so many levels—I can't shut him out of my life. I work for him. I've loved him my whole life. How would we overcome this?"

"I—I don't know. But I know I'd like to try. Don't you even want to try?" He grasped her gently and pulled her stiff body into his arms. "Please. I just found you. I don't want to lose you, Hope."

Her hands trailed slowly up his arms and gripped onto his biceps as her body began to tremble. Her head rested on his chest, her hair falling forward to mask her face, but her heart was being broken in two. He raised his hand to brush her hair away, but before he could, she wrenched free of his hold and turned away.

"No, no! I'm sorry. I can't do this. It's already too hard." She turned and, upon seeing his grief-stricken expression, felt the very last of her composure begin to crumble. "Goodbye, Gage." And then she fled from the room, the door slamming behind her as she dashed to the elevators.

She was expecting him to follow so wasn't sure if she was relieved or more shattered when he didn't. As she climbed into the elevator and pressed the button for the lobby, she began heaving great breaths of air to try to contain the sobs threatening to break free. How many more times was she going to have to grieve the loss of this perfect man? She wasn't sure how much more her heart could take.

The elevator doors swished open, revealing a lobby that thankfully held only a handful of guests. She cast her head downward as she walked to the front desk and asked the clerk to please summon the car service for her, explaining one was on call for Yorke. Yes, she even had a car on call when needed, another perk of being Robert Yorke's daughter. She laughed out loud, causing the desk clerk to look at her in concern. Yes, she had all the perks of being a Yorke, including the extra bonus of losing the man she had fallen in love with because of it.

Gage's heart thudded to a halt as he watched the door to his suite slam shut. *How in the fuck did this just keep getting worse?* Instinctually, he knew he should go after her, but common sense told him to let her go. She'd been through enough, and chasing after her would only cause her more pain right now. He'd told her things about her father that he knew she needed time to process.

He dropped down onto the closest sofa and reached for the nearly full tumbler of vodka he had poured for Hope, draining it in one gulp. He got up to make another when he heard his phone chirp, indicating an incoming message. His pulse quickened as he walked into the bedroom and pawed at the pockets of the slacks he had discarded earlier, looking for his phone. It finally tumbled out and thumped to the floor on its own.

Bending to retrieve it, he was surprised to see a text from Ben. He sighed in disappointment because he really wanted that message to be from Hope. Swiping the screen, he clicked on Ben's name to read the message.

Just saw Hope leave. I'm in the lobby bar if you want to talk.

. . .

He scratched his chin as he processed the message. *Did he want to go down to the bar? Talk about Hope? Drown his sorrows? All of the above?* Fuck it. He was going to go stir crazy if he stayed put in this room all night, especially with the smell of her on the sheets to haunt him. He pulled off the shorts and t-shirt he had on and switched them for a pair of jeans. Walking into the bathroom, he took the dress shirt he, and Hope, had worn earlier and, pulling it on, began fastening the buttons. *Was it crazy that she only had it on for half an hour, but it made him feel like she was wrapped around him?*

He took the elevator down to the lobby and made his way to the bar, finding Ben seated by himself at the far end, a crystal tumbler of warm, brown liquid in front of him. Gage sat down on the empty stool beside Ben and nodded. "Hey."

"Hey. Wasn't sure if you were coming down." He motioned for the bartender. "You want something?"

Nodding, he addressed the bartender. "I'll take a Ketel One, rocks. A double."

"You want to talk about it?" Ben took a slow sip of his drink, brows raised as he peered over at Gage.

The bartender came over, placed a fresh tumbler in front of Gage, and walked away. "Not really." He raised the glass to his lips, the ice cubes clinking as he took a large drink.

"Yeah, guess that wouldn't be the manly thing to do." A light chuckle followed Ben's reply.

"Nope." Another clinking sip of his drink followed. "I'm

surprised you're still here. I know you hate these things as much as I do."

"There was a girl." He grinned broadly as he shrugged.

"Isn't there always?" Gage shook his head and smiled sardonically. "Hopefully, your night ended better than mine."

"She's playing hard to get, but the feisty ones usually do."

"Did you at least get her name?"

"Yep. Jill. Gorgeous blonde. Owns a spa or something. She came with Drew's friends, Mika and Rae."

"Good luck with that." He scoffed lightly. "I've got my own blonde to worry about."

"Since you brought it up, man, Hope didn't look too happy when I saw her leaving. I didn't even know you knew each other. When did that start?"

Gage shrugged and blew out quickly. "Eight days ago."

Ben's hand slapped loudly on the bar as he let out a loud guffaw. "Eight days? Shit. What'd you do? Love her and leave her?"

He shook his head while running a hand over the scruff lining his chin. "Something like that." He turned his head and looked at him seriously. "I think I fell in love with her."

"That's a bad thing?"

"Isn't working out to be a good thing."

Ben's hand clapped onto his shoulder and squeezed lightly before letting go. "I'm sorry. Genuinely. Can I do anything?"

"You know her father, right?"

"Yeah, sure. I mean, I guess so. Our families have been friends for as long as I can remember, so we've spent time together. He the problem? Doesn't want her dating some military grunt?"

Shaking his head, he told Ben, "I wish it was that simple. There's some history, and it's not the good kind."

"She feel the same way?"

He raised his eyebrows. "About me? You mean, is she in love with me?" He nodded his head. "Yeah, I think she is. But she loves her father more. And what daughter wouldn't?"

"Her mom's gone. Did you know that? A car accident a few years ago."

He scoffed and took a large gulp of his drink. "Yeah, that's the fucking problem."

"Wait, what? You lost me, man."

Gage raked his fingers through his hair and grimaced. "Never mind. It's a long story, and I just don't want to go there again."

"Another drink then?"

"Yep, might as well."

Looks like drowning his sorrows wins for the night.

Chapter Twenty

Hope looked at the clock on the dashboard and noted the time. Ten-fifty. Her father would most likely be home and possibly already in bed, but she needed to confront him and didn't want to wait another minute.

"Could you take me to my father's apartment instead, please? Do you need the address?"

"No, ma'am. I'm familiar with it."

"Wonderful. Thank you."

She could call him. Her phone was in the pocket of her skirt, but no. She wanted to catch him off guard. Any warning she gave him would just give him more time to fabricate more lies, and she'd had enough of those. Several minutes later, the driver pulled up in front of her father's building. A doorman appeared and opened her door, helping her out of the car. She thanked the driver and made her way into the foyer of the building.

"Do you know if Mr. Yorke is in?" she questioned the doorman.

"I believe he is, ma'am. His secretary came around earlier, so I suspect he's working. Would you like me to call up?"

"No. Thank you, though. I'll just go directly."

The doorman tipped his hat and returned to his station as she made her way to the elevator. She punched the arrow pointing up and stepped inside the elevator once the doors slid open.

She clenched and unclenched her hands nervously as the elevator climbed to its destination, wondering if she was making the right decision in coming here and confronting him. Perhaps she should have waited until she wasn't so angry and confused. The elevator slowed to a stop, and the doors swished open. It was now or never she supposed and, bracing herself, stepped into the short hallway and went to his door.

Her shoes clicked on the marbled floor of the otherwise silent space as she unlocked the door and made her way toward the living room. Lights were on, so she assumed that perhaps he was reading, or possibly even in his office working. When she didn't find him in the living room, she turned and started down the hallway to his office.

She could see the door was slightly ajar and the light on, and felt some relief at finding him in his most likely hiding spot. As she got closer, she pushed the door wide and smiled when she saw her father sitting at the desk, head buried in some paperwork.

"Daddy?"

His head snapped up in surprise before a wide smile broke across his features. "Hope, darling! What a nice surprise." He stood and came around the desk, pulling her into his arms in a warm embrace before pushing her back and looking at her. "You're all dressed up. And you look like you've been crying? What's wrong?"

She pulled herself out of his arms and stepped back, nodding. "We need to talk."

His brows creased, and all humor left his eyes. "This sounds serious."

"It is." She turned and started back down the hallway. "Let's go sit in the kitchen, okay?"

When they entered the kitchen, she walked to the coffee machine and smiled when she felt a warm pot already waiting. She pulled a mug out of the cabinet for herself. "Do you want a cup?"

"Yes, that sounds nice, dear."

She already knew he was going to say yes but asked anyway. He loved his coffee and usually always had some close by. She poured them both a cup and handed his to him black. She added her usual sugar and cream and couldn't help but feel a slight pang in her heart, frowning when she remembered how Gage would tease her about the lack of coffee in her coffee.

"You're worrying me. Please, tell me what's on your mind."

She sat down at the counter next to him and smiled sadly. "Faith Flynn is on my mind."

His eyes narrowed, and he shifted uncomfortably. "I thought we had already discussed this."

"We didn't discuss the part about you having an affair with her. Or the baby she was carrying when she died. Your baby, Daddy. My half-sister."

He turned visibly pale, and the hand holding his coffee began to tremble. He set the cup on the counter and let out a heavy sigh. "Oh, darling. I'm so sorry you had to learn about any of that. Would you believe me if I said I only kept it from you to lessen your pain?"

"No." She shook her head angrily. "I think you hid it from me because it was easier for you and you knew I wouldn't forgive you."

"Will you let me explain?" He reached for her hand and pulled it into his. "Please?"

She stared at him for a long time before responding. Perhaps it was only seconds, but it felt like minutes before she finally did. "I do want to hear what you have to say, but I honestly just don't know if I will believe anything you tell me."

He nodded, his eyes sad and understanding. "And I accept that possibility. I know it's of my own doing."

She nodded this time. "Okay then, I'm listening."

"I loved your mother very, very much, Hope. As hard as this may be for you to believe, Faith was the first and only time I ever strayed in all our years together."

One eyebrow arched high as she tilted her head in doubt, but she remained silent.

"Your mother was extremely busy with her charities, and I suppose I was, too, with my work. We stopped spending any real quality time together." A flush crept up his neck to his cheeks in obvious embarrassment over the topic of discussion. "She was always tired, and no longer wanted to go out, travel, or even just spend time together."

He glanced over at her sheepishly. "I'm sorry, this isn't a very comfortable thing to discuss with my daughter."

"Daddy, I'm a grown woman. I can handle it. Go on." She waved her hand in the air to indicate he should move along.

He nodded. "I was just peaking over my mid-fifties, and I suppose feeling a bit sorry for myself, thinking perhaps the best part of my life was over. And then, out of nowhere, in waltzes this intern. She's young, and she's beautiful and so eager. I began to notice that her eyes followed me every-where when we were in the same space."

"Faith?"

Her father nodded with a sad smile. "Yes, Faith. I was so flattered that this beautiful, young woman was interested in me, and God forgive me, I acted on it. I invited her to work on a cover project with me and kept her late one night. It started out slowly. Dinners here and there. A concert. Then, finally, well, I'm sure I don't have to spell it out for you."

"No, I'm sure you don't, but I'd like you to. I need to understand exactly how her and Mother ended up in that car together."

His sad eyes locked onto hers as he nodded grimly. "I know, and I'll get there." He stood up then and, taking his mug, walked to the coffee pot and poured himself another. He lifted the pot to her in question, but she shook her head no. He stayed on that side of the counter and began to speak again.

"This continued for several months. I can't say for sure if anyone at the office caught on or not. We were very discreet there, but I saw her three and sometimes four nights a week. I used one of the corporate apartments, so it was easy to just say I'd been working late or at a dinner engagement. I even took Faith to Miami with me for a conference I had."

"Yes, she wrote Gage and told him about the trip. She told him she had fallen in love and that you shared her sentiments." A scowl dressed her face as she looked at him. "Did you, Father? Did you love her?"

He smiled wistfully but shook his head no. "There are a lot of things I regret in this life, but that may be one of the biggest. I took this young girl and used her to make myself feel better, not realizing the horrible impact it would have on her. I was a fool to not realize how naïve she really was. I loved the time I spent with her. I loved the way she made me feel young again. I loved how such simple things brought her joy and made me feel like a man again. But, no, I didn't love her. Your mother is the only woman I've ever loved."

"But you got her pregnant. Did you really ask her to abort the baby?"

Shame flashed across his face, and she knew instantly what his answer was. Sick to her stomach, she gasped, "Father, you didn't!"

He moved to sit next to her again and grasped one of her hands in his. "Only in the purest moment of shock and weakness. Shortly after we came back from Miami, I realized that I was making the biggest mistake of my life and needed to end things with her. I asked her to meet me at the apartment, where I told her I had to let her go, and, of course, I apologized for any hurt I was causing her."

He grimaced at the memory but continued. "She was heartbroken. Said she didn't know how she was going to live without me and professed her love to me again and again. And, honestly, I was devastated as well but only because it hurt me to know my selfishness had caused her so much pain. She didn't deserve it. She really didn't."

Hope could see that her father was genuinely saddened about the grief he had caused Faith, which only caused her feelings about the whole matter to become more unstable. "Is this when you found out she was pregnant?"

"No, not for another week or so. And, in that time, I confessed everything to your mother. I had committed the worst betrayal to her and our marriage that I could, and she deserved to know the truth."

Her eyes widened in surprise at his admission. "You told Mother? So, she knew about the affair?"

He closed his eyes briefly and shook his head as if he himself couldn't believe the outcome of his confession. "She didn't know until I told her, and, of course, she was hurt and angry, and in a way only your mother could, she was forgiving."

"Mother forgave you? Really?" Disbelief laced her voice.

He scoffed as if he himself still couldn't believe it. "She did. She said that, after twenty-five wonderful years, she could forgive me one indiscretion. God only knows why, but your mother loved me."

"Because she was amazing, Daddy. How could you have ever stopped seeing that?" Her voice was quiet and filled with disappointment.

He patted her hand, a knowing frown on his face. "I know, baby girl. I know. Don't think that I haven't asked myself that a hundred times."

"This still doesn't explain the pregnancy and the car accident." She wasn't letting him off the hook that easily.

"It may have been five or six days after I had ended the relationship with Faith that she came to my office one late afternoon. She told me she was pregnant and was already over four months along. I was shocked, to say the least, and I confess, at first, I didn't believe her. I assumed it was a ploy to try to prolong the relationship, and I know I said things that were awful and unkind. I made her leave, and instead of feeling sympathy, I admit, I only felt anger."

"Well, I suppose that's a natural reaction, but you must have considered it was possible that she really was pregnant?"

He nodded. "Of course, and she confirmed it the next day when she came by again, this time with a sonogram of the baby. I was shocked into submission, to say the least. And also at a loss. I honestly had no idea what to do or say, so I asked her to come back the next evening so we would discuss it."

"And did you?"

"I went home and told your mother. That was even harder than telling her about the affair."

Hope's hand went to her mouth as it dropped open in

surprise. "My God, Daddy! Poor Mother! She had to deal with all of this. She must have been so mad."

"Yes, she was furious. But only at me. She felt only compassion for Faith and insisted we do whatever needed to care for her. She demanded she be there the next day to also speak with Faith. So, that leads us to the night of the accident."

"That was the next night?"

"Yes, your mother came into the office around three, and around four, Faith arrived. I'm not going to lie. It was quite a scene. I don't think it was until that moment that Faith realized I truly had no intention of leaving your mother, no matter her current condition. I know it broke her heart, too, which is something I'll never, ever forgive myself for."

He let out a long sigh, his face heavy with grief. "Your mother was the one to finally calm Faith down. She spoke to her like she was her daughter and not her husband's mistress, assuring her we would help. She made sure Faith understood that we would be in the baby's life no matter what; we wanted to be there, whether it was to help her raise it or adopt it if she didn't want to keep it."

He looked at Faith then, his eyes sad and moist at the edges. "Your mother was an amazing woman. If I had any idea what was going to happen…"

Her father drew in a deep breath and nodded once as he finished his story. "Your mother insisted on taking the car and driving to Faith's to get some of her things. She was going to have her come back and stay at the house so we could care for her properly. The weather was turning, but your mother scoffed at me and reminded me that she grew up driving in snow storms. I wasn't quite comfortable with the arrangement, but I daren't argue with her at that point. I decided to stay back at the office and wrap up a few loose ends, and then I was going to meet them back at the house later."

"So, it really was just an accident that killed Mother and Faith?" she asked incredulously.

He nodded slowly, eyes full of despair. "And your sister, Hope. You would have had a little sister."

"Oh, Daddy." She fell into his arms then as he wrapped them around her and held her tightly. "How could you have kept this from me?"

He murmured over the top of her head, "I'm so, so sorry, darling."

Chapter Twenty-One

F*our Months Later*

Gage flinched and swore under his breath as a firm knock on the door broke his concentration. He was trimming a photograph, prepping it to be matted, and he'd just sliced off a fraction too much. He slammed his fist down on the table and drew in a deep breath to calm himself. It didn't take much to anger him these days.

He dropped the knife on the table and walked to the door. Three more hard knocks sounded on the other side just as he grabbed the handle to pull it open. "Chill the fuck out! I'm com—"

His eyes widened in surprised disbelief, and if it was

even possible, his boiling point rose to a precarious edge. "What do you want?"

"I'd like to talk if you have a moment." He watched as Robert Yorke shifted uncomfortably in his doorway. "I think it's long overdue."

"I'd say it was about six years overdue." Shaking his head in disgust, he stepped back out of the doorframe and motioned for Robert to come inside. As much as he didn't want to be within ten feet of this man, he was curious as hell to hear what he had to say.

"Thank you." He walked past and gasped out loud, "Oh!"

Gage regarded the man's shocked expression and shrugged. "It's the only way I can be close to her." His gaze swept around the room, following the path Robert's eyes took. Every wall was covered in framed photographs of Hope—her laughing, looking straight at him, on the bridge, of them on the hill together, her sleeping. She was everywhere.

The older man's eyes fell back on him. "You love her."

"Does it matter?"

"Very much indeed." He walked further into the room, unbuttoning his coat before shrugging it off. He moved to set it over a chair and then pulled another one out to sit in. "May I?"

Gage waved his hand in the air to indicate he should do as he pleases. "What can I do for you, Mr. Yorke?"

"Please, call me Robert."

"I'm not planning on getting friendly enough to be on a first name basis with you, so let's just keep this formal."

He watched a small frown appear on the man's face as he

nodded curtly, and Gage was surprised at how amenable the man was attempting to be, causing his curiosity to grow. "Again, what do you want?"

"I'd like to explain. Something I should have done a long, long time ago."

Scoffing loudly, Gage moved to stand across the table. "Why now? I begged you years ago, and you would tell me nothing."

"Something I regret very much and have come to learn was the wrong thing to do. I thought I was protecting the ones I love, but, well, it seems I've done much more harm than good." He motioned toward the chair Gage was leaning on. "Won't you sit down? This might take a little while."

Curiosity getting the best of him, and his desire to finally have more information about what happened to his sister, had him sliding down into the seat. "I'm listening."

Gage focused all his attention, his emotions swirling in different directions, as Robert Yorke detailed the same story he had told Hope back in October. When he was done, both men sat in silence, each taking the other in across the table.

"Why are you finally telling me this now? Why couldn't you have told me this years ago?"

A long, exhausted sigh fell from Robert. "I truly thought I was protecting my wife. She didn't deserve to have her name dragged through the mud because her husband's lover was in the car with her... Let alone, her husband's pregnant lover. Can you imagine what the newspapers would have done if they'd gotten hold of that?"

"Do you actually think I would have gone to the papers

if you'd told me and my family the truth?" Gage spat out angrily.

"At the time, I couldn't see past my own immediate family and needs. I had no idea that you knew your sister and I had a relationship, or that you knew the baby was mine. Then, when you confronted me, I did what I always did in that situation. I lied, and for that, I'm sorry. I'm very sorry that I've caused you and your family the pain I did. But, son, it *was* an accident. We all lost that day, and I do know that it may be hard to swallow, but I, we, would have done the right thing by Faith. My wife would have it no other way."

Gage stood up and paced around the room, not sure where this conversation was supposed to be headed. He turned and faced Robert. "What are you looking for then? Forgiveness?"

"No, not today. Maybe someday, though. I know this is something that may never come, or at the very least, something that has to be earned."

Gage watched as Robert stood and walked to one of the photographs of Hope. She was in the canoe and staring out at the water, a look of serenity on her face. "She's beautiful, isn't she?"

He nodded but said nothing.

"She hasn't quite forgiven me yet. But, I think, well, I hope, perhaps maybe soon. She did let me visit her for Christmas." Gage watched as the older man turned back to face him. "She's living up at the house in Vermont now. Did you know that?"

He shook his head. "She's not in New York?"

He watched as Robert walked back to the table, pulling his coat off the chair he had hung it on earlier, and began to put it on. "No, she left in November. She's writing, if you can believe that."

A small smile appeared across his lips. "I can, actually."

"You should go see her, son. My secrets and lies have caused enough heartache. Don't let it come between what you obviously still feel for her."

Gage watched him silently, absorbing everything he had just learned, and could only nod his head.

Robert approached him and extended his hand. "Thank you for listening. I truly wish that I had done this sooner, but I hope having the complete story eases some of your pain."

He stared down at the hand stretched out before him and, without conscious thought, reached out and grasped it firmly in his own, pumping it once before letting go. He watched the man who had scarred so much of his life walk out his door and wondered what he was supposed to do now.

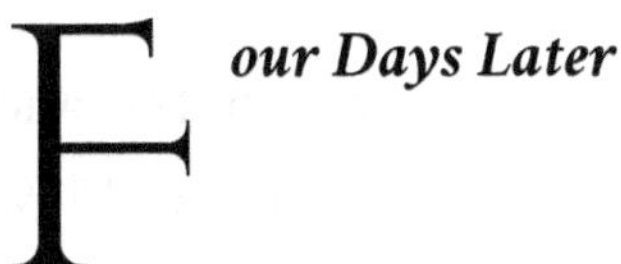

F*our Days Later*

.   .   .

Hope watched as a light snow fell outside and left another clean layer of white, fluffy powder on the already growing drifts at the window. It had been snowing most of the morning, but curled up under a blanket in front of the fire left her little cause for concern.

She was working on a coming of age story that had always prickled in the back of her mind. Writing had always been a long-term goal for her, but given all the events that had occurred over the last few months, the timing of things had been turned up a notch. Lord knows she had enough money, between the trust fund her father had established for her long ago and the money she had earned while working.

Thinking of her father and all they had gone through over the last few months drew a long sigh out of her. She missed him, but she still needed more time to forgive him. And she knew she would eventually. Time did, in fact, heal all wounds. Well, maybe not all wounds. Thinking about Gage still caused an ache in her heart that compared to a knife piercing through its very core. But at least she didn't cry anymore whenever she thought of him. That was progress, she supposed.

She turned her attention back to her computer and stared again at the words she had typed out over the last few hours. She was about to begin typing again when a knock came from the door. Placing the laptop on the cushion beside her, Hope lifted the covers off her as she rose from the couch. She slid her feet into the comfy pair of fur-lined slippers lying next to the couch and scuffled to the door.

Walter always liked to stop by and check on her when the snow began falling. Opening the door, she yelped in surprise when the last person she expected to see stood before her.

"Gage! Oh my God! What are you doing here?"

She watched as a huge smile bloomed across his face, the adorable crinkles she'd come to love lifting and lining the corners of his bright green eyes.

"Are you going to let me in? It's fucking freezing out here."

She stepped back and waved her arm, indicating for him to come in, her mouth still hanging open. He entered and shut the door behind him, stomping his snow-covered feet on the rug. He looked up at her and winked. "I know you hate when I drip over all your things."

"I don't. I just... What are you doing here?" she stammered, having a hard time getting anything else out.

"Well, I would think that would be obvious. I came to see you." He unwrapped the scarf around his neck and then removed his jacket, his eyes never leaving her as he did. Finally, he pulled his boots off and stood in front of her. "I've had enough of this."

"Enough of what?" Her face held a bewildered expression as she tried to process the fact that he was standing in front of her.

"Enough of not seeing you." Then he swept her into his arms and crushed his mouth to hers in a searing kiss. It took only a second for her to recover before her arms wrapped around his neck and she was kissing him back. She clung to him as if he were her next breath, her fingers clutching onto the hair that fell over the nape of his neck. His hand moved to her face, his fingers caressing her cheek gently, before he pulled his lips from hers, his forehead resting against hers as their heavy breaths collided.

"I've missed you so much, Angel."

He leaned forward and pressed his lips to hers again but only for a moment before pulling away again. "I want to take you upstairs right now and strip you naked, but…"

"But we should talk."

He nodded against her forehead. "We should talk."

She let go of him and stepped back, her arms wrapping around herself in protection. She went to turn, but his hand reached out and threaded through her hair and around her scalp, pulling her close, as he bent down and pressed his lips to hers again. She whimpered when his teeth nipped her bottom lip, and he let go once again and backed away.

"I'm sorry," he breathed out. "I just had to do that one more time."

She turned and walked back to the living room, him walking beside her. She went and sat on the couch and couldn't help the smile that formed when he stopped to put more wood on the fire before he joined her.

He pointed to the laptop. "You're writing?"

Her brows furrowed quizzically. "Yes, how did you know?"

"Your father."

Eyes widening, she stammered, "My father?"

He nodded. "He came to see me a few days ago."

She asked again, not sure if she heard him correctly. "My father came to see you?"

"Believe me, I was just as surprised."

She moved to adjust the blanket over her body nervously. "What did he want?"

"To tell me the truth, I guess, about your mother and Faith, about what happened the night of the accident." He ran a hand through his damp hair and shrugged. "Better late than never, right?"

She frowned. "And, so, you thought you should come see me now?"

He shifted so he could move closer to her and rested his hand on her thigh. "He told me to come see you."

"He what?"

He nodded. "He said he'd caused enough heartache and if I still loved you to come see you."

"Oh." She stared at him, dumbfounded by her father's actions, watching as he shifted uncomfortably. "And do you?"

"Do I what?"

"Still love me?" It came out on a whisper.

He shook his head. "Do you really have to ask?"

"Gage, what about your family? They could never accept me."

"I flew here from Pennsylvania. I spent the last two days with them, telling them what your father shared with me, but mostly telling them all about you."

"And they are okay?"

He shrugged. "It's a lot for them to accept and understand in a short amount of time, but, yes, I think they'll be okay. More than anything, they know you are a victim in everything that happened."

"What about you?"

His eyes narrowed. "What about me?"

"Will you be okay with everything that's happened? Can you be with me, knowing who my father is and what he did?"

A scowl crossed his features and then vanished. "I was angry at your father, at your family, for a really long time. Mostly because I wanted to understand what happened and wanted answers. Your father finally gave me some of that when he spoke to me the other day. Am I ready to be sitting across from him at a family dinner?" He shook his head. "Not yet, but I don't want to kill him anymore. Over time, I'm hopeful it will get easier."

She turned her head and watched the flames lick over the logs, teasing and tickling the wood that would soon be burned to dust. She was so afraid opening her heart up to Gage again could very well cause her the same fate.

She twisted her head back to him as he moved to slide up against her waist on the couch. "Hope, over the last four months, all I've done is think of you—every time I walked into a coffee shop and heard someone order more cream than coffee, every time I saw a white Range Rover drive down the street, or saw a woman with long blonde hair, or any time I smelled lemons. Do you know that you smell like lemons?"

She shook her head, eyes locked on his.

"And every single time I closed my eyes, all I could see was you—in my arms, lying back in the grass, kissing your lips, tasting your skin. I heard your laughter in every smiling picture I took of you. You've invaded my soul. You want to know if I still love you?"

His hand moved up and cupped her cheek, and he brought his face even closer to hers. "Baby, I never stopped." Then, their lips were fused together as one as tears rolled down her cheeks.

Chapter Twenty-Two

Gage rolled onto his side, dragging Hope with him as he slid out of her, a groan of protest falling from her lips as he did.

"God, I missed this the most."

"You always were a little bit of a minx, but you're going to have to give me a little break. That's the third time in two hours. I'm not a machine, woman!"

"Well, I haven't had any visitors since you left. What do you expect?" She giggled, hoping he didn't forget their conversation about past lovers so many months ago.

He leaned up on his elbow and gave her ass a playful smack. "There better not have been. I better be the last visitor in this bed ever again!"

"Ow!" She snuggled into him after his spanking. "You better be able to say the same, Mister!"

He bent his head and feathered kisses against her silky tresses. "Only you, my angel. Only you."

He smiled as he felt her sigh contently and then grinned mischievously when she rolled over onto her back, giving him a perfect view of her beautiful body. He stroked a hand over her breast, cupping it and swiping a thumb over the hard nipple.

"Is it my imagination or have these gotten bigger?" He bent over and sucked the peak into his mouth, swirling the hard tip around his tongue, eliciting a loud moan from her.

"You better stop that or be ready to suit up for round four."

He released her nipple with a soft pop and grinned up at her. "Food. We need food if you're going to make me do this again."

She giggled and whacked him on the head softly. "Oh, I'm sure this is pure torture for you."

He watched as she sat up and then stood beside the bed. Laughing lightly, he pointed at her softened middle. "I think, now that I'm here, we're going to have to get you eating healthy again. Let me guess, all pasta and wine diet?"

Her face paled as she looked down at the little paunch that now graced her normally slim frame before looking back up at him. "I'm not getting fat." She caught her lower lip between her teeth, biting down hard, and gave him a shrug. "I'm pregnant."

His heart literally stopped in his chest. His eyes flew open wide as they shot back and forth between her belly and her eyes, in shock. "You're—"

"Pregnant." She finished the sentence for him and placed a hand over the round bump protectively.

A thousand questions spun in his head, but the one

feeling he could not dismiss was pure and utter joy. She was pregnant with his baby. Holy shit.

And then, as realization sunk in, his euphoria wore off. His brows furrowed, and he frowned. "Were you going to tell me?"

She nodded her head and sat back down on the bed, covering his hand with her little one. "Yes, I just didn't know how. I was so afraid of what it would mean. I didn't want to force you to be with me, or be a part of my family, knowing how much you despise my father."

"When? When would you have told me?" He wasn't certain if he believed she would have ever told him, a cold wave of fear slicing through him.

"I actually have the plane reserved for Monday next week. I have an ultrasound scheduled that day to learn the sex. I was going to come see you directly after. I swear it, Gage."

He stared at her, trying to read every emotion displayed in her pleading eyes.

"Please, believe me. I would never deny you this right, especially after what my father did." She then laced her fingers through his and moved his hand over the soft spot on her belly. His eyebrows shot up at the realization that his baby was growing under his hand. "This is our baby, made only from love. I'm not going to let anything that's happened before ruin this."

He brought his gaze up to meet her wet one and grinned widely. "We're having a baby. You're having my baby?"

She nodded, small tears trailing down her cheeks. "I'm having your baby."

~

"Will you stop pacing already?" Hope was lying on the exam table, hands folded over her middle, watching Gage eat up the space in the small office with his wide strides.

"How much longer are they going to make us wait?" he huffed out, coming to a halt and crossing his arms over his chest.

No sooner than the words were out, the door swung open, and a young woman entered the room. "So sorry to keep you waiting, Miss Yorke." She stopped then, her eyes landing on Gage. "Oh, you must be the father?"

Hope's heart soared when she saw his face light up at the reference, and any fears she had about him not wanting this baby evaporated. "That's right. I'm the father. Gage Flynn." He had stretched his hand out, but the tech just nodded and walked to the table where she lay.

"Come this way, Mr. Flynn." The tech pointed to the table beside the bed. "You'll be able to see the screen from there."

He moved over and clutched Hope's hand in his. She was surprised to feel it was clammy and cold. She squeezed it gently and looked up at him. "Hey, you okay?"

He nodded down at her. "Excited."

"Okay, this might be a little cold." The tech had lifted her shirt and was squirting light blue gel onto her belly. She placed a white tool onto the goo and started sliding it around. All of a sudden, through the static, they could hear quick thumping.

"That's the heartbeat," the tech said, smiling as she looked up at them. "It's nice and strong. It's right at a hundred-thirty beats a minute."

"Is that good?" Concern laced Gage's voice.

The tech smiled at him. "That's very good."

Hope looked up at him, beaming. The tech pointed out the actual heart and took measurements of the baby's body, head, and spine, again noting everything looked perfect. "It looks like you are nineteen weeks along, making conception right around the beginning of October. Do you want to know the sex?"

"Yes!" Hope and Gage both answered in unison, causing the tech to laugh.

"It makes it easier when parents agree. You'd be surprised how many don't." She swirled the instrument around on Hope's tummy for a moment and then stopped. She pointed to an area on the screen that, quite frankly, just looked like a v shape to her and smiled.

"You're having a daughter."

Epilogue

age watched in wonder as Hope appeared over the edge of the hill like the angel he had always known her to be. The simple white dress she chose to wear billowed out behind her as she gracefully traipsed to stand beside him, her face golden and dewy in the fading sunlight. He grasped onto her hand and leaned down kissed her cheek, whispering, "You look stunning."

It was exactly one year ago on this very hill that they both realized they had fallen in love, and neither of them could think of a better place to exchange their wedding vows. Of course, this time, they had an audience, so there would be no lovemaking in the grass afterwards to consummate their union.

He looked over his shoulder and smiled at his parents. His mother was holding his lace-covered daughter, cooing to her softly. "Hush, Alana Faith. This is Mommy and Daddy's moment to shine."

She had arrived ten days early, on July seventh, and came out kicking and screaming. They thought it only fitting that she also fell somewhere in the middle of their own birthdays, being born on zero-seven-zero-seven. They had decided to move back to the city, him moving into Hope's apartment, so Gage could continue his work, but they spent as much time as they could at the house in Vermont. Her book was being published next month, and she had already begun penning another.

On the other side of Hope stood her brother and her father. This hadn't been an easy feat to achieve, given his parents' presence, but the love both sets of parents had for their children superseded all other feelings for that day.

They only wanted their immediate family present for this part—where they expressed their love, their devotion, their commitment to forever. There would be a big reception in Burlington with all their friends when this was over, but this part of the world, the top of the world, was just for them.

And they lived happily ever after…

Dear Reader,

I hope you loved Losing Hope! I have another stand-alone you might enjoy just as much. It's called Catching Chase, and I have a sneak peek coming up right after this.

If you did enjoy this book, I would be so grateful if you left a review. It means everything to an author to hear your thoughts and to help other readers decide if they would like to read.

Thank you so much for reading, and I hope to see you again soon!

xo Michelle

Catching Chase

I step out of the Uber onto the sidewalk in front of the hotel I'm staying at, pausing to tilt my face up to the sun. It's only seventy degrees, but much more pleasant than I'm used to in January. I smile through the heat warming my cheeks, knowing from a conversation I had earlier with my office, that it's snowing in New York. You can bet I didn't register one complaint when they asked me to come to Los Angeles for the week.

I hum out a contented sigh, open my eyes, then turn to push through the revolving door into the lobby, my heels screeching to a halt as I absorb the sight before me. Men. In suits. Lots of them. All large in stature. Before I even have time to blink to make sure I'm not dreaming, a hard body slams into me from behind, a yelp of surprise bursting from me as I fly forward. Every one of those well-dressed men turn their heads in my direction when the folders I'm holding spill out of my arms and scatter across the marble floor in front of them.

"For Christ's sake Chase, don't you look where you're going?" One of the men in the lobby shakes his head, stretching his arms out to point in my direction. "Look what you did to this poor woman."

It's then, when the heat from his response blows against my neck, that I register the strong fingers gripped around my waist, tightening as they shift me into a stable position. "I obviously didn't expect anyone to be standing smack in the middle of the doorway asshole." His hold releasing as he moves beside me, his gaze locking onto mine, his voice lowering. "Pardon my language." This clearly directed at me and not the other man, as his attention stays focused on me. "Are you alright? I'm sorry about that. I didn't see you."

Jesus, Joseph, and Mary. This man is gorgeous. And has manners to boot. I blink twice, making sure I haven't walked into some kind of dream. I nod and hum out something resembling "uh-huh", too tongue tied by surprise and his beauty to speak any real words. My cheeks heat and in an effort to hide my embarrassment, I bend to begin retrieving my scattered files. He follows suit, sweeping papers into a neat pile, his fingers brushing against mine, startling me again, my eyes darting up to his. I feel my head tilt as the most unique colored irises I've ever seen lock onto mine, leaving me mesmerized. They remind me of the caramel squares I used to eat as a child. The ones often found at the grocery store, individually wrapped in clear cellophane, that you could buy in bulk. The thick, dark lashes framing them are in such contrast to the light color, it's difficult to say with certainty if they are hazel, brown or gold. The dark flecks of green and brown scattered around his pupils actually provide a shimmering effect when he blinks, dazing me further.

One side of his mouth quirks up in a smile, dimples somehow appearing, even though there's a thick beard lining his face, my heartbeat stuttering in response as he speaks, his voice lower this time. "I really am sorry."

I finally snap to my senses and say something to the poor man. "It's my fault. I shouldn't have been standing in the doorway. So, I fear I'm the one that actually owes you an apology."

I move to push myself off the floor at the exact same time he leans forward to help me up, our foreheads meeting in the middle with a hard thunk, stars appearing in my vision from the impact. I slap a hand over the spot where we collided and let out my second yelp of the day as I straighten, glaring at him as I do. Laughter rings loud from the hoard of men watching our every move from the lobby, a few comments thrown out referring to smooth moves and what a jackass my would-be-gentleman is.

"What in the hell is wrong with you?" I hiss. I've had enough and finally lose my patience. "Are you always this much of a klutz?"

His brows shoot north, his entire body jerking back in shock. "I'm the klutz?"

"First you run into me, and then you smack your head into mine, so yes, I'd say you're lacking the basic motor skills that usually keeps one in their own lane."

One of the men in the crowd lets out a low whistle then laughs. "Guess she must have seen you play in last week's game, eh, Chase?"

He points in the direction of his friend. "Shut it White." His glare shifts to me, the files he's still holding thrust toward me. "Here."

I snatch the pile from his outstretched fingers, add them to the stack I'm holding, then stride purposely away in the direction of the elevators.

"You're welcome." His voice booming over the noise my heels are making against the marble floor, sarcasm lacing every syllable.

I halt, then whirl around, my eyes squinting at him in disbelief. "You're welcome?" I take several steps needed to close the gap between us, the blood boiling in my veins as I approach. "Are you kidding me right now?" His mouth opens to speak, but before he can get a word out, I seethe between clenched teeth. "You slam into me, spill my files everywhere, then smack your head into mine, all while your little frat brothers watch on the sidelines, and you expect me to say thank you?"

His mouth quirks up in a lazy smile, his head shaking once back and forth before he speaks, quietly, so only I can hear him. "Well aren't you just a little spitfire?"

"What did you call me?" I splutter, taken aback by his response, so completely opposite of what I was expecting.

His reply comes only after his lips form a wide smile, his caramel gaze practically sparkling with mischief. "You've got one fiery little temper on you." I stare at him, not sure if it's because his eyes have put me into some kind of trance, or because I'm just not sure how to respond. Either way, it doesn't matter, because he keeps speaking. "My mom always said never argue with a girl with spitfire spirit. Now I understand why."

I squint suspiciously at him, trying to figure out what his angle is. One minute I want to strangle him, and the next, I find myself looking at his lips wondering what they would feel like against mine. And what kind of guy quotes his mother for God's sake? "Yeah, well, your mother was right."

"I know." He smile grows broader. "Which is why I'm not saying another thing."

"You're weird." I state, matter-of-factly, my eyes traveling the length of his well-dressed frame before looking him in the eyes again. "Even if you are cute." Before things get even stranger, I give him one final shake of my head, turning my back to him as I walk into the elevator. As the doors start to close, I spin around, a reluctant smile breaking free when I realize he's still rooted in place, still watching me. When the doors clunk together, I roll my eyes and laugh out loud. "Weirdo."

Want more?

Grab it over on my webpage:

www.authormichellewindsor.com

About the Author

Michelle Windsor is the author of over a dozen steamy, contemporary romances filled with alpha males and even stronger females. She has achieved both Amazon and Barnes & Noble International Best Seller status, and was awarded Best Contemporary Romance Writer by Passionate Plume Ink in 2019. Her first book, The Winning Bid, was nominated for the Summit Indie Book Awards by Metamorph Publishing in 2017, and continues to be her best-selling book to date.

Michelle is married with three grown children, and lives north of Boston in the type of suburban neighborhood you read about in sweet romance books, (not hers)! When she's not working on another book, you can find her spending time with her husband, hanging out with her three sisters, or snuggled up with her three cats, yes three, watching a movie or reading a book.

Keep up to date with Michelle on her web page:
https://www.authormichellewindsor.com

Also by Michelle Windsor

The Winning Bid

The Final Bid

The Ultimate Bid

The Auction Series Collection, Bid Books 1 - 3

Love Notes

Catching Chase

Tempting Secrets

Tempting Tricks

Tempting Justice

Tempting Teacher

Tempting Nights Box Set Collection, Books 1 - 3

Just One Christmas

Taking Flight